AMERICA'S
WHODUNIT QUEEN

CHARLOTTE MACLEOD

Don't miss any of the MacLeod excitement!
Charlotte MacLeod's two mystery series—
starring campus criminologist Professor Peter
Shandy and private detective/art investigator
Max Bittersohn and his sleuthing wife Sarah
Kelling—are available in these Avon editions:

The Peter Shandy Mysteries

Rest You Merry
The Luck Runs Out
Wrack and Rune
Something the Cat Dragged In
The Curse of the Giant Hogweed

The Max Bittersohn/Sarah Kelling Mysteries

The Family Vault
The Withdrawing Room
The Palace Guard
The Bilbao Looking Glass
The Convivial Codfish
The Plain Old Man

The Plain Old Man

CHARLOTTE MACLEOD

AVON
PUBLISHERS OF BARD, CAMELOT, DISCUS AND FLARE BOOKS

The entire cast of characters in this book is imaginary, and Pleasaunce is
no more a real place than Gilbert & Sullivan's Ploverleigh. One unexpected
element of reality did turn up, though . . . there really are people named
Kelling. The author, who makes every reasonable effort to avoid using
actual people's names, had believed for some years she'd coined the name
herself. Now she finds there are two brothers trying to draw up a genealogy
of the apparently very few real Kellings living in this country. In return
for being made an honorary Kelling, the author has promised to forward
any data readers may be able to give. Please address letters to her personal
attention in care of the publishers, and mark "Kelling" on the envelope.

AVON BOOKS
A division of
The Hearst Corporation
1790 Broadway
New York, New York 10019

The Doubleday edition contains the following Library of Congress Cataloging in
Publication data:

MacLeod, Charlotte.
    The plain old man.

    I. Title.
PS3563.A31865P6   1985   813'.54

First Avon Printing: October 1986

For Alice,
Priscilla, and Sackville

THE SORCERER

An Original Comic Opera

Words by W. S. Gilbert, Music by Sir Arthur Sullivan
Presented by the Pirates of Pleasaunce
Mrs. Beddoes Kelling, Director
Dramatis Personae

Sir Marmaduke Pointdextre (an Elderly Baronet)	John Tippleton
Alexis, His Son (of the Grenadier Guards)	Parker Pence
Dr. Daly (Vicar of Ploverleigh)	Sebastian Frostedd
Notary	Charles Daventer
John Wellington Wells (of J. W. Wells & Co., Family Sorcerers)	Ridpath Wale
Lady Sangazure (A Lady of Ancient Lineage)	Emma Kelling
Aline, Her Daughter (Betrothed to Alexis)	Jenicot Tippleton
Mrs. Partlett (A Pew Opener)	Martha Tippleton
Constance, Her Daughter	Gillian Bruges

Music by The Beddoes Kelling Memorial Orchestra
Scenery by Sarah Kelling Bittersohn and Guy Mannering

Letter from Miss Mabel Kelling
to Mrs. Appolonia Kelling:

Dear Appie,

I presume you expect to be thanked for the gift which I have not yet been able to identify. Never let it be said that I am remiss in my social duties. Speaking of which, you had better not plan on staying with me overnight when you come to attend Emma's latest venture into amateur theatricals. You know she will be miffed if you don't allow her to play lady of the manor offstage as well as on, though I'm not sure where she's going to park you if Sarah's still there. It looks to me as if she'll be around a good deal longer than Emma expects. Sarah claims that new husband of hers is off on another of his so-called business trips. Surely even you can read between the lines!!!

Anyway, they are up to their eyeballs over there with the play, or comic opera as I believe those Gilbert & Sullivan things are properly called. The plot, as far as I've been able to make out, deals with a boy and girl who are foolish enough to become engaged to each other, and their parents (a widow and widower respectively) who wish to be engaged but for some never-explained reason are not.

There is also a silly young thing who is chasing after the vicar, he being at least twice her age. She has a mother who is listed on the program as a pew opener. This presumably refers to the period when the gentry had themselves shut into high-walled pews at church so the common folk couldn't see what they were up to during the service. Since you are so totally inept at keeping a story straight, I thought I might as well explain in advance what this one is all about, rather than get hissed at for information all through the performance as generally happens.

After the usual tiresome overture, a chorus of village men and maidens (!!!) sing the usual sort of unintelligible nonsense about how happy everybody is today because Aline (the girl) is getting bethrothed to Alexis (the boy). Then the pew opener and her daughter come on looking as grumpy as we shall all, no doubt, be feeling by then. The daughter (Constance) tells her mother (Mrs. Partlett) that she is in love with the vicar, who doesn't care for her. Needless to say, the vicar then appears, declaiming that the girls aren't chasing him any more now that he's old and fat instead of young and handsome. The mother tries her hand at matchmaking and fails, naturally, this being only the beginning of the show.

They go away, no doubt to everyone's relief. The boy (Alexis) and his father (Sir Marmaduke) come on and are congratulated by the vicar (Dr. Daly) for quite some time. You know how ministers run on. These three go away and on comes Aline with the rest of the girls. She sings a song about marriage having its disadvantages as well as its alleged advantages, as if one had to be told. Then the mother (Lady Sangazure) and prospective father-in-law (Sir Marmaduke) enter and they all sing a lot of gibberish about one thing and another.

At last the lawyer appears with the bridal contract. Instead of reading out the terms in a sane and sensible manner, the young people go ahead and append their signatures to the unread document, while the chorus stands around loudly applauding this totally rash and senseless act.

Eventually they all leave the stage except Alexis and Aline. Alexis expounds some ridiculous theory that everybody ought to marry everybody else with-

out distinction of rank. Aline, like a besotted little
ninny, agrees with him. He then tells her he has
resolved on obtaining a potion which will make all
those villagers who have shown a reluctance toward
lawful wedlock (though no doubt sufficient forward-
ness in other directions!) fall in love with one another.

Aline protests, but of course he doesn't listen—
men never do—and they go off to one J. Wellington
Wells, a sorcerer (hence, I assume, the name of the
production) to get the potion. He subjects them to a
lot of mumbojumbo, no doubt as an excuse to jack
up the price, then sells them the potion, which he
puts into a large teapot Alexis has brought with him.
Alexis, mind you, being the son of a baronet (Sir
Marmaduke)—can you picture a baronet's son carrying a large teapot, unwrapped, through the streets
of London? Perhaps this is meant to add a touch of
humor.

In any event, they take the pot to a tea party
which Sir Marmaduke (the baronet) is giving to cel-
ebrate the betrothal. Too cheap or too broke to buy
champagne, I suppose—they always are, aren't they?
Alexis, who appears to have no moral principles
whatsoever (he being the hero, you will recall) tricks
the vicar into making tea in the aforementioned teapot and gets everybody to drink some except himself,
Aline, and the sorcerer, who has somehow wangled
an invitation to the affair. At this point, mercifully,
we have an intermission. I expect the Girl Scouts
will be peddling pink lemonade and cookies as usual.

Having developed acidosis in support of whatever
good cause Emma happens to be supporting at the
moment—after that fire-engine business I quit
trying to keep track—we go back to our seats, if we
can find them, and watch everybody wake up and
fall in love. First the members of the chorus conduct
a sort of mass wooing, then Constance (the pew open-

er's daughter, as you've most likely forgotten by now) enters arm in arm with the lawyer, moaning that she has suddenly lost her feeling for the vicar (which wasn't getting her anywhere anyway) and fallen madly in love with this plain old man as she describes him and as he will certainly be, since I understand Emma's old flame Charlie Daventer is to play the role, assuming he can shake off his booze-induced gout in time.

Moving on less rapidly than one might wish, Constance (see above) bewails her plight at quite unreasonable length with Alexis, Aline, and the chorus all getting into the act. Eventually Alexis and Aline are left alone. Alexis starts nagging at Aline to drink the potion also and thus become his willing slave for life (you will notice that *he* never offers to drink it and become *her* willing slave!!!). During the ensuing quarrel, Sir Marmaduke comes along engaged to the pew opener (Mrs. Partlett). Lady Sangazure, who will of course be played to the hilt and then some by Emma herself, falls in love with Mr. Wells (the sorcerer), who rejects her, he being the only one so far who's shown a lick of sense despite his odd profession.

Then Aline drinks the potion, not in front of Alexis, which would have been at least plausible, but just in time to meet Dr. Daly (the vicar) who is wandering along playing a flageolet (a penny whistle, in plainer terms) and complaining that everybody is now engaged to somebody and nobody is left to marry him. At that point he comes face-to-face with Aline and they fall in love.

Well, of course Alexis is furious at being jilted even though he's brought it upon himself, and goes whining off to Mr. Wells to undo the spell. It turns out that the only way this can be done is for either Alexis or Wells to die. If you can make sense of that, you will show greater acumen than I've ever found cause to credit you with. Anyway, Wells gets thumbs-down from the assemblage and disappears through the trapdoor, assuming it's in working order this time.

At last all the couples switch around and get suitably mated, another comic touch, one assumes, and sing something about strawberry jam and rollicking buns. All this is supposed to add up to a highly diverting evening. I shall take my knitting with me.

Yrs. aff.,
Mabel

Chapter 1

"He's ugly and absurdly dressed, and sixty-seven nearly. He's everything that I detest, yet if the truth must be confessed, I love him very dearly."

Sarah Kelling, who was now in fact Sarah Bittersohn but had found one didn't get out of being a Kelling through a mere nuptial technicality, sang because she was happy. Sloshing bucketfuls of paint on yards and yards of canvas was glorious work. This was going to be a shrubbery in front of which the vicar would pour his pretty stiff jorum of tea. Sarah decided she'd try her hand at a *Prunus glandulosa* as soon as she'd finished the *Lagerstroemia indica*. She was using one of Aunt Emma's seed catalogs for a reference, and it was having the usual heady effect. The glorious difference here, though, was that a scene painter could make her shrubs bloom as grandly as the ones in the photographs, while a gardener seldom could.

"You very plain old man, I love you dearly."

Had her husband, Max, been around, he could have deduced that the Pirates of Pleasaunce were doing *The Sorcerer* this year. As it happened, Max had just set off for Belgium on the trail of a purloined Picasso when Emma Kelling sent out her distress signal. Emma was Lady Sangazure this time around. Last year she'd been Katisha in *The Mikado*. The year before that, she'd been the Fairy Queen in *Iolanthe*. And she'd been great. She always was.

Emma Kelling's contralto voice was like her person, rich and full-bodied. She'd been a handsome young woman when she'd married the late Beddoes Kelling. She was a handsome woman still, and meant to stay that way.

"I tell myself," she observed to Sarah, "you're not getting older, you're merely getting blonder. Is my bustle on straight?"

Emma rather went in for innovative costuming. She'd played Little Buttercup in a middy blouse and black sateen gym bloomers, she'd played Lady Jane in a batik tutu and the Duchess of Plaza Toro in a court train eight yards long that had created no end of problems among the chorus; but she'd never sung Lady Sangazure in a bustle before, and felt it was high time she did. Sarah couldn't have agreed more.

"It's superb. That huge purple bunch over your behind will strike the perfect balance beside Sir Marmaduke's paunch."

Emma had never quite lost her schoolgirl giggle. "Jack Tippleton has put on more than a bit over the winter, hasn't he? For goodness' sake don't let on you've noticed or he'll stalk off in a huff and then where shall we be?"

"Right where we are now. Surely you don't believe for one second that Jack would give up a chance to swank around in a velvet coat onstage and show off his profile?"

As far as Sarah knew, John Armitage Tippleton had spent his entire sixty years and then some standing around looking handsome. If he hadn't been cursed with money and position, he might have become a movie star. However, on those relatively few occasions when Sarah had seen him, he'd never appeared other than totally satisfied with being John Armitage Tippleton.

Sarah wasn't so sure about Martha Tippleton. This was the first time she'd been involved with Aunt

Emma's coterie on a level where she could get to know them as individuals instead of just hands holding cocktail glasses or teacups at Emma's innumerable parties. Jack's wife was cast this time as Dame Partlett. Sarah wondered how long Martha had been playing that role.

"She will tend him, nurse him, mend him, air his linen, dry his tears."

And while Martha was doing all those useful tasks, Jack would be off in a corner with the sweet young thing who was playing Dame Partlett's daughter, Constance, making a horse's necktie of himself. Max wouldn't have said necktie. Sarah began painting little pink hearts on her bush in place of blossoms.

"What a charming touch, dear," said Emma. "Absolutely right for the betrothal scene. You might do them a weentsy bit larger so the people in the back rows will be able to see they're hearts. We do manage to fill the hall, as a rule."

She didn't have to tell Sarah that. To begin with, most of the Kelling clan always showed up. Counting the sisters and the cousins whom they numbered by the dozens, not to mention the brothers and the uncles and the aunts, they made a fair-sized crowd in themselves. Sarah herself had been coming to see the Pirates ever since she could remember, walking over to North Station with her parents to catch the train for Pleasaunce and be picked up at the station by some relative or other, or riding in Great-uncle Frederick's Marmon—Kellings never parted with their cars until they absolutely had to and often not then—with Cousin Dolph sweating at the wheel and Great-aunt Matilda doing the driving from the back seat. Later, she'd gone in the Studebaker, alone in the back seat while Aunt Caroline rode up front with Alexander. Year before last she'd come by herself, a widow with a broken arm. Last year had been the best. Max had driven her out in his elegant car, singing excerpts from *The Mikado* all the way. He'd made an unconvincing Yum-Yum, but his "Tit-Willow" had been magnificent.

Sarah hoped desperately that Max would make it back with the Picasso in time for the performance. Only three days to go, and the scenery not even finished. This was an unheard-of situation. Normally Aunt Emma would have everything ready to roll by now. However, the production had been visited by a string of calamities. A week ago the barn in which the Pirates had been storing their scenery for eons past had been struck by lightning and burned to the ground. Then Henry Holst, who'd painted most of the flats in years gone by, had begun complaining that he was too old to climb ladders any more, and proved it by falling and spraining his thumb with half the windows in Sir Marmaduke's mansion yet to go. Aunt Emma had called Max's departure for Belgium an act of Providence and demanded that Sarah come at once to finish the mansion and do the landscaping.

Sarah had meant to spend the time landscaping her own mansion, or at least going out to ponder yet a while on what, if anything, could be done with the white elephant she'd fallen heir to at Ireson's Landing. Since she loved Aunt Emma dearly, however, she'd borrowed a pair of overalls from Cousin Brooks and hastened to oblige. This time she'd driven herself so that she'd have a means of getting back to Boston in a hurry if Max came home and wanted her there, or if the atmosphere at Aunt Emma's became too fraught, as it sometimes did at rehearsal time.

The Pirates' actual performances were always held in a rented auditorium. However, it was in Emma Kelling's Late Robber Baron mansion with its sixty-foot drawing room that preparations went on, sometimes for months, until the costumes were fitted, the props collected, and the cast rehearsed.

The orchestra was never a problem to Mrs. Kelling. Beddoes Kelling had formed his own years and years ago so that he'd have an excuse to go on playing the tuba after graduation forced him out of the Harvard Band. After his untimely and still-much-lamented death, Emma had kept the group together as darling Bed would have wanted her to.

They weren't a highbrow lot. They were none of them all that fussy for Brahms and Debussy, but liked best to play Strauss and Lehar for Waltz Evenings, or to tootle all the airs from that infernal nonsense *Pinafore,* or *Ruddigore,* or *The Yeoman of the Guard* or, needless to add, *The Sorcerer.* At the moment, Emma's Bechstein was half buried under flutes and clarinets, nor could you get at the keyboard without first tripping over a bass viol, a concert harp, or Beddoes Kelling's own tuba, played these days by his son and namesake as an act of filial piety but kept at Emma's house out of consideration for Young Bed's own wife and family.

Over the years Emma had worked out her own ways of coping with the multifarious details of putting on a Gilbert & Sullivan production. As it happened, the bedroom Sarah always had when she came to visit was also the one in which certain costumes were hung after they'd been taken out of their boxes and pressed. It would have been unthinkable to object to Aunt Emma's filing system, so Sarah ducked meekly to her bed each night under a clothesline strung with lengths of phosphorescent muslin in which the fiends of flame and fire would be draped when the sorcerer conjured them up. She didn't mind; she only hoped the trapdoor wouldn't stick when he had to disappear in the final scene.

That had happened once when she was about seven. With the necromancer trapped halfway through, she'd screamed out, "Squish him down," to the delight of the audience and her ever-after embarrassment. Kellings believed in getting full value out of their jokes as well as their clothes and their cars; she wondered how many of the relatives would ask her if she meant to squish down the Sorcerer this time. Cousin Dolph already had, of course, twice.

Well, these things were sent to test us, as Cousin Mabel was wont to say. The rest of the family were more inclined to assume Cousin Mabel had been sent to test them.

Mabel would be at the performance, no doubt. She'd never missed one yet, nor had she ever said a kind word about it afterward. Too bad Mabel couldn't be given a swig of J. W. Wells's all-purpose love potion.

"Give me that love that loves for love alone," Sarah caroled, reaching for a different bucket of paint.

"Why love for love alone?" her aunt wondered.

"I was thinking of Cousin Mabel," Sarah explained.

"How noble of you, dear. I always try not to. Oh glory be, here comes Charlie. And Gillian's nowhere in sight, after she'd promised faithfully to be here on the dot of four. I can't for the life of me see why people come panting after parts and then won't ever bother to be on time for rehearsals. Give her a buzz, will you, and see if she's on her way? I'll take Charlie through his stage business in the meantime so he won't feel abused and neglected."

Charlie—Charles Daventer, to give him his due—didn't have a great deal to do in his role as the Notary, except to get Aline and Alexis duly signed and sealed and to be fallen in love with temporarily by Constance Partlett. Charlie would much rather have been fallen in love with by Emma Kelling, for whom he'd nursed a hopeless but on the whole agreeable passion since the spring of 1937. However, he was willing enough to submit to Constance's unflattering blandishments, since Emma wanted him to.

The Notary didn't have to sing well. A croak would suffice, but the croakings had to come in the right places, and therein lay the rub. Shortly after rehearsals began, Charles Daventer had been laid up with a bad go of gout in his left big toe. Emma's man, Heatherstone, had been conscripted to understudy the Notary's role, which he'd read from the book in a careful monotone, pending Charlie's recovery. That was all right for the other players, but of no earthly use to Charlie. He'd kept insisting he'd be well in time to do his part, so Emma hadn't dared replace him with one of the men from the chorus; and in fact there was none of them dry and snuffy, dim and slow, ill-tempered, weak, and poorly enough to have handled the role convincingly. Now here he was, back in trim and raring to go and where was their Constance? Really, it was annoying of Gillian.

Sarah let the phone ring, but Gillian/Constance didn't answer, so they had to suppose she must be on her way. Emma gave Charlie a sisterly kiss and a weak whiskey and water and started running him through his lines for the betrothal scene, of which he had precisely four. Sarah, painting her bushes amid a sea of tarpaulins in the vast, glassed-in room that Emma called her sun parlor, could hear them pegging away. Now they'd gone on to the chorus that followed, Emma singing most of the parts while Charlie made frog noises half a beat behind. At last, when her own voice began to wind down from the strain of doing soprano, alto, tenor, and bass all at the same time, Emma called, "Sarah, come in here."

Sarah stuck the brushes she'd been using into a can of water so the acrylic paint wouldn't dry in the bristles and break Henry Holst's heart, and obeyed. "What is it, Aunt Emma?"

"Charlie wants to do 'Dear friends, take pity on my lot.' I'll be the orchestra, you sing Constance's part."

"Me? I'm no singer."

"Nonsense. You've been warbling it to yourself all afternoon. You know the lyrics better than Gillian does. Here." She thrust the score into Sarah's reluctant hands and fought her way between the harp and the tuba to the Bechstein. "And a one and a two."

The duet between Constance and the Notary was one Sarah particularly liked. The melody made no unreasonable demands on her modest vocal endowment, and the words appealed to her sense of the absurd. She gave it her best shot. Charlie came in right on the button, with due lugubriosity. Emma was impressed.

"Capital, both. You've caught it nicely. Shall we try it again?"

"Why not?" said Charlie. "I was pretty good, wasn't I?"

Sarah was reminded of Tartarin de Tarascon singing the role of Robert le Diable. Oh well. Her arms were tired from painting, anyway.

"Dear friends, take pity on my lot. My cup is not of nectar. I long have loved, as who would not, our kind and reverend rector."

"Why, Sarah, what a delightful surprise." The voice was a well-modulated baritone. "I never knew you cared."

Emma banged her hands down on a C-major chord. "Sebastian, sit down and shut up. We were going along nicely till you barged in. Let's start again, Sarah."

Sarah didn't much relish having to perform in front of Sebastian Frostedd. She couldn't think of much about him she did relish, for that matter, even though he was easily the best voice in the company. He might well be the best actor, too. If even a few of the scurrilities Dolph and Uncle Jem had told her about him were true, Sebastian was grossly miscast

as the Vicar. Still, he carried off the role as if he'd
been in churchly orders all his life.

His role seemed not to be the first thing he'd carried off. According to Dolph, some of Sebastian's so-
called business deals ought to have landed him in
jail ages ago, if his relatives hadn't kept bailing him
out. There was the Frostedd name to think of. Besides, as Dolph pointed out, no matter how black his
other crimes, Sebastian could always be counted on
to vote the straight Republican ticket.

Perhaps it was part of Sebastian's stock in trade
to look more like a clergyman than a crook. He was
a smallish, roundish man with a little mouse-fine
grayish hair surrounding a shiny pink pate and a
blandly agreeable face. He wore thin beige or gray
cashmere vests under his discreet sports jacket at
rehearsals and could have passed himself off, if not
as a man of the cloth, at least as the assistant head-
master from one of the better girls' boarding schools.
Maybe he had, for all Sarah knew. She personally
would never trust any daughter of hers, assuming
she were to have one, with a man like Sebastian
Frostedd. She turned her back on him, making sure
she'd got the concert harp between them, and went
back to bar one.

By the time she and Charlie Daventer got through
their number, they'd accumulated quite an audience.
Alexis the brave and the lovely Aline, also known
respectively as Parker Pence, son of the second flute
and the kettledrums, and Jenicot Tippleton, daughter of Sir Marmaduke and Dame Partlett, had arrived. Parker was a nice boy, Sarah thought. He was
following in the parental as well as the aval footsteps
by playing glockenspiel in the Harvard Band. He
also sang tenor with the Glee Club and was seriously
considering a career with the Handel and Haydn
Society plus a bit of investment brokerage on the

side. The side that liked to eat, presumably, the rewards for choral singers being more aesthetic than financial as a rule.

Sarah thought Jenicot something of a brat, perhaps out of jealousy, as Sarah herself had never been given the chance to be bratty. Jenicot was a natural redhead, though she'd be playing Aline in a marvelous blond wig that was even now perched on a block in one of the upstairs bedrooms. Not Sarah's this time. Her costume was there, too: a birthday cake of mauve ruffles, pink rosebuds, and baby-blue satin ribbons. Jenicot had the willowy height to carry it off. She hadn't had the requisite candy-box prettiness to start with, but she would have by the time Emma Kelling got through with her. Already she'd acquired enough decorum to sit still on the sofa and applaud with the tips of her fingers as they left the piano.

"I didn't know you were doing Constance, Sarah. What's happened to Gillian?"

"Nothing, I hope. She's supposed to be on her way here. I was just filling in."

"You didn't do too badly for your first try," young Alexis condescended to tell Sarah. "Who's your voice teacher?"

"I never had one. It's just that my father used to sing in Cousin Percy's madrigal group and I had to fill in sometimes when one of the trebles didn't show up."

"You mean hey nonny nonny and all that garbage?" said Jenicot, reverting to type.

"I like doing madrigals," her swain told her with no little severity. "They're fun. How's the scenery coming, Sarah?"

"Messily." She held up the paint-stained hands she hadn't been given time to wash, and Emma took the hint.

"Go get cleaned up, Sarah. It's teatime anyway. Charlie, you'll stay of course."

"Might as well, now that I'm here."

He really was a plain old man, Sarah thought. Cousin Brooks had some photographs he'd taken of a California condor in molt. Once Charlie Daventer got on his stage makeup and claw-hammer coat, he was going to look a great deal like that condor. She wondered whether Gillian's missing the rehearsal might be one of those Freudian slips Cousin Lionel and his ghastly wife, Vare, were always going on about: things you forget because you never wanted to do them anyway.

Gillian was a better soprano than Jenicot, in Sarah's opinion. It might well gall her to be paired with ugly old Charlie instead of the dashing though dim-witted hero. However, it was Emma who'd done the casting and there'd been no question in her mind as to which of them would be given the soprano lead, considering that Jenicot was a Tippleton well on her way to becoming a Pence, and Gillian Bruges was quite something else again.

Emma Kelling must have known she was asking for trouble when she took on an attractive unknown who'd shown up at the tryouts with the vaguest of introductions from some neighbor or other. Jack Tippleton had never yet got through a production without making a play for one of the actresses. He'd almost been forced to pick Gillian this time, simply because the only other featured performers in the cast were his daughter, his wife, and Emma herself. Jack wasn't inclined to bother much with members of the chorus, though he was quite willing to settle for a Pitti Sing or a Fleeta, and often had.

Maybe that had been another factor in Emma's apportionment of the roles. If the affair got around to the point of throwing scenes and flouncing off in a huff, Emma wanted to make sure it was not one

of her lead singers who flounced. She'd lost her An-
gelina that way, one time when they were doing *Trial
by Jury* with Jack as the Judge. It had happened the
night of the dress rehearsal, as Sarah recalled. Aunt
Emma, trouper that she was, had taken up another
notch in her corsets, crammed herself into the wedding dress, and burlesqued the role to its ultimate
limit. She'd brought down the house, but it had taken
a lot out of her. Not even Emma Kelling would care
to repeat such an experience as that one. Sarah hoped
to goodness she wasn't faced with it now.

Chapter 2

For the present, though, it appeared they had no crisis. Gillian showed up shortly after Heatherstone had brought in the tea, apologizing all over the place and telling some horrendous tale of a blocked gas line in her car. She was set to rehearse and the tiniest bit miffed when she found out they'd been able to manage without her. Charlie—magnanimously, considering the state of his big toe—said he wouldn't mind running through their number again. Then Jack Tippleton arrived, ostensibly to pick up Jenicot. Gillian decided Charlie ought not to strain his gout any further today and started feeding cucumber sandwiches to Jack.

Jenicot took a dim view, as daughters will. "Daddy, don't eat that. You know what cucumber does to your gall bladder."

Brattishness pure and simple, yet Sarah found herself warming toward Jenicot. "Here, Jack," she said, "have a ladyfinger and tell us about your gall bladder."

That had not been a clever move; Sarah had forgotten what a strange effect she was having on men now that she was happily married and decently dressed. If Jack had a mustache, he'd be twirling it. Gillian Bruges was noticing and resenting. Oh dear, surely she hadn't been taking this posturing old goat seriously.

It was possible, Sarah supposed, that Gillian didn't

see Jack as a posturing old goat. He was still handsome in an elder statesmanish sort of way and his
technique, if one were susceptible to that sort of thing,
must have acquired a high polish after so many years
of practice. Maybe Gillian was into father figures,
as Max's nephew Mike would say. In any event Sarah
decided she'd better keep a respectable distance
from now on between herself and Jack Tippleton's
gall bladder. She could rather easily picture Gillian
throwing up a second-best part, and there was no
way Aunt Emma could sing Constance as well as
Lady Sangazure.

Luckily a diversion presented itself in the person
of Guy Mannering, son of the English horn. Guy was
an art student at Worcester. Lately he'd taken to
rushing back to Pleasaunce after classes so he could
paint scenery with Mrs. Bittersohn, she being a
glamorous and sophisticated older woman who might
reasonably be expected to sympathize with a young
aesthete's higher yearnings. Sarah was not at all
sure she did, but she assuredly valued Guy's height
and muscles for juggling the flats around. She'd nail
him for that later; right now he wanted to talk art.

"What do you really think of the Romney?" he
was asking her in a low, confiding tone meant to be
suave but somewhat blurred by a bite of scone he
hadn't quite finished swallowing.

Sarah looked up at the life-sized portrait over her
aunt's fireplace. Complete with birdbath and white
dove, it depicted a strong-featured woman in her
middle years costumed as Venus, albeit in a far more
covered-up style than Venus is usually shown wearing. Roses being appropriate to the goddess and flat-
tering to full-figured ladies, the artist had painted
in a great many of them, some twining around the
birdbath, some wreathed in her hair and pinned to
her bosom, one apparently being fed to the dove. Her
first thought was that she hoped to goodness Aunt

Emma wasn't intending to will the portrait to her. With its wide, gilded baroque frame, the thing must measure at least six feet by eight, and where on earth would she ever find room to hang it in the kind of house she and Max were planning? Her second was that she'd hate to have the responsibility for anything that valuable. Her third was that Romney must have had either a highly developed sense of humor or none whatsoever. Her fourth was that she adored it. It was the fourth that she offered to Guy.

He looked at her in ill-disguised horror. "You do?"

"Oh yes, it's so much like Aunt Emma."

"Oh." Guy chewed that over for a moment, along with the last of his scone. Then he gave her a kind, paternal nod. "Yes, I can see the resemblance. Was it her mother or somebody?"

Art history evidently wasn't one of Guy's current subjects. It was as well Emma Kelling hadn't heard his question.

"Actually, no," Sarah replied. "Romney died in 1802. This was Ernestina, the wife of an Alexander Kelling who was some kind of attaché to the Court of St. James's shortly after the Revolution, when John Adams was minister. I believe they didn't last long. She and Abigail didn't get along very well."

"Abigail Adams always felt she was slighted in London," Sebastian Frostedd, who was sitting next to them, put in. "But I can't imagine anybody had the gall to slight Ernestina. Then of course the Kellings were rich and the Adamses weren't. That's bound to create ill feeling."

"Surely not with Abigail Adams," Sarah protested. "I thought she'd have been above that sort of thing."

"Nobody is."

Sebastian stretched out a hand to the muffin stand Heatherstone was passing around. A cabochon ruby in the massive gold ring he was wearing caught a

deep crimson spark from the candles the servant had
lighted, for the sun was beginning its downward slide
and the sky had grown overcast. April showers again
tonight, Sarah thought. She hoped it would be fine
tomorrow. Guy and a couple of his friends were coming early in the morning with a truck to move Sir
Marmaduke's mansion from the sun parlor over to
the auditorium. She and Guy ought to be out there
right now finishing those bushes instead of dawdling
over the teacups.

Still it was pleasant to dawdle and actually there
wasn't all that much left to do. In a way Sarah was
sorry they'd had only the one set to paint. That didn't
mean her work was over. As decorations for the auditorium Emma wanted great massed arrangements
in osier baskets, for which complicated foundations
would have to be constructed out of plastic dishpans,
chicken wire, tape, and that spongy green stuff which
takes up water and keeps cut flowers fresh.

Emma's plan was to have Sarah cut and arrange
the greens during the day tomorrow, then go out
toward sunset and pick vast numbers of tulips and
daffodils from the garden. These would be immersed
up to their necks in water overnight for some esoteric
reason Emma had learned at the garden club. The
following day they'd be taken out of the water all
fresh and turgid, another garden-club word, and
popped in among the greenery. Getting the baskets
ready sounded like a day's work in itself.

Two days. One to pick and one to pop. Sarah was
dreamily trying to remember how many for the foyer,
how many for the refreshment area, how many for
the orchestra when she realized Ridpath Wale had
joined them, coming on little cat feet as was his wont.

Ridpath was their John Wellington Wells, another
exemplar of Emma Kelling's flair for casting. He
projected to a dot the image of brisk businessman-
cum-sorcerer. The first time Sarah had watched him

rehearsing his potion-brewing scene with Alexis and
Aline, she'd got a flash of sudden terror that he was
going to pull off a workable spell. At the moment
he'd joined Sebastian and Guy in front of the Romney, and was gazing up at the late Ernestina as if
he wouldn't mind trying to put a spell on her.

"Gad, that's a beautiful thing," he sighed. "I'd give
my eyeteeth to own it."

"Well, offer Emma a few hundred thousand and
see what she says," Sebastian told him. "What's the
going rate on Romneys these days, Sarah?"

"My husband could tell you better than I. I do
know Madam Wilkins paid forty thousand pounds
for the painting exactly like this which she bought
for her palazzo back in 1907. Unfortunately, hers
turned out to be a fake."

"Emma's is authentic, of course." Ridpath managed to turn a declarative sentence into a mocking
question.

"Absolutely," Sarah informed him, turning a simple adverb into a pretty crisp rebuke. "In the first
place, this portrait has never been out of the family
since the original Ernestina brought it home. In the
second, we've had it authenticated up, down, and
sideways by about twenty different experts over the
years, mainly because of that copy at the Madam's.
Mrs. Wilkins tried to claim Romney painted more
than one portrait of Ernestina, the way he did of
Lady Hamilton, but that's absurd. Romney was a
strange sort of man, but he wasn't eccentric enough
to keep on immortalizing the Kelling jaw. Anyway,
Ernestina wasn't in London long enough. Abigail
Adams saw to that, I expect."

"Forty thousand pounds, eh?" said Sebastian. "In
that case, I'm afraid you'll have to boost your offer
half a million or so, Ridpath."

The Sorcerer laughed. "Can't manage it this week,

I'm afraid. Well, ladies and gentlemen, are we going to rehearse or are we not?"

"I'm not." Jack Tippleton got up. "Come along, Jenicot. Your mother will be wondering what's kept us."

"Oh, I hardly think so," drawled the brat. "Thanks for the tea, Mrs. Kelling. Coming with us, Parker?"

"I've got my car, thanks."

"Goody," cried Gillian Bruges. "You can give me a lift back to the garage and save me another horrendous cab fare."

Neither Jack Tippleton nor his daughter looked any too happy at this prospect. Regrettably, Parker Pence did. Maybe it didn't mean anything. Parker was a good-natured young fellow, otherwise he mightn't be able to hit it off so well with Jenicot. Nevertheless, Sarah had full confidence she'd soon be hearing some wonderment among the cast about what Gillian Bruges thought she was up to.

The whole thing was silly, Gillian was as much too old for Parker Pence as she was young for Jack Tippleton. Those winsome ways of hers, Sarah had decided at their first meeting early in the week, were more the result of long practice than of girlish exuberance. Well, it would all blow over, no doubt, once they'd done the show. In the meantime, she had her own attendant squire to command.

"Come on, Guy," she said, "let's finish that last flat."

Guy Mannering was only too happy to follow Sarah out to the sun parlor. If he'd had any hopes of engaging her in aesthetic chitchat instead of painting bushes, though, he was soon disabused of them. Sarah could be a first-class drill sergeant, having got in plenty of practice on Edith, her late mother-in-law's cantankerous maid, during her traumatic first marriage. They did in fact manage to get done with the hearts and flowers before Sarah had to change for dinner and Guy to go and do whatever it was he did when he wasn't painting scenery at Emma's.

If he hadn't been wearing paint-stained jeans he might have got asked to dine with them, but Emma, whatever her other impetuosities, was too much a lady of the old school to allow for that. Sarah wasn't surprised to find out she'd invited Charlie Daventer to stay, though; it would have been unusual if she hadn't. What did surprise Sarah was that Ridpath Wale was still with them. He generally had some other engagement.

She put on a peacock-blue silk dress she'd picked up in Phoenix—being married to Max was giving her wardrobe a cosmopolitan flavor—and went down prepared to be bored stiff by endless talk about stage technique. To her surprise she found them still talking about the Romney. Rather, they kept coming back to it, especially after they'd returned to the drawing room for their after-dinner coffee.

Ridpath wanted to know how so large a painting had been fitted into that monstrous frame, and how they'd ever got it off the ship and out to Pleasaunce.

Sarah knew that. Ernestina had in fact been trundled over the roads in a brewer's wagon. Emma told the story, and made an engaging comedy of it. As to the mechanics of the painting, there was no way she could extract much entertainment from them. The canvas was simply tacked in the customary way to a heavily braced wooden stretcher which in turn was held into the frame by large wood screws.

"The thing can be taken apart easily enough, then?" Ridpath remarked.

"Oh yes, it's not hard, merely awkward because of its size and weight. We have Ernestina down every ten years or so for cleaning."

"Looks to me as if she's about due for another bath," Charlie grunted.

"I'm afraid you're right," Emma agreed. "The oil

heat leaves a film, you know, and I'm sure the smoke from the fireplace doesn't help, even though we had those glass doors put on for that very reason. Heatherstone gets up on a ladder and gives her a wipedown with a damp cloth every so often, and we flick off the cobwebs once a week with a marvelous longhandled feather duster I picked up in England ages ago. It's begun to molt, poor thing, and I don't suppose it accomplishes much. There was a nice man in Springfield who used to come out, but I'm sorry to say he's died. I must call up the museum and see if they can recommend somebody."

"The fellow who cleaned my Sargents did a satisfactory job, I thought," said Ridpath. "I'll ring him up tomorrow, and have him drop by to give you an estimate."

"Not tomorrow, please, Ridpath. I must get this show over before I tackle any more projects. We have enough confusion around here already. I do hope we shan't have a clash of temperaments over Gillian Bruges. That girl is a minx. I suppose I should have known better than to take her on in the first place, but she does make a divine Constance."

"If it weren't Gillian it would be somebody else," Charlie reminded her. "We all know what Jack Tippleton's like. I can't imagine why Martha hasn't walked out on him long ago."

Ridpath Wale shrugged. "Because we all know what Martha's like, I suppose. Emma, my extrasensory perception tells me you're about to offer us a brandy."

"Right over there on the tray. Help yourself, won't you? I don't know where Heatherstone's got to. He's worn to a frazzle, poor man. I must say I'm none too spry right now, myself. Pour me just a splash while you're about it. Charlie, you'd better not. We don't want your poor toe flaring up again. Sarah, how about you?"

"None for me, thanks." Sarah reluctantly got up from the gold-brocaded easy chair she'd been enjoying. "I must stir my stumps. I promised Cousin Frederick I'd run over this evening and see his new suit. It's the first one he's bought in thirty-two years."

"What if Max calls?"

"He won't, not tonight. He's left Belgium and is on his way to Helsinki."

"Good heavens, whatever for?"

"Don't ask me. Is there anything you want me to take to Cousin Frederick?"

"Only my love. Tell him Heatherstone will save him a seat for the show and he's to wear his new suit. None of this business of letting it hang in the closet for the next ten years so the moths can bite pieces out and it won't look vulgarly new."

Charlie Daventer snorted. "Huh. At Fred's time of life, he can't have ten years left to wait."

Sarah was annoyed enough to remind Charlie that he himself had been Cousin Frederick's classmate, but she forbore. She merely said her good-byes, remembering not to drop a curtsy to her elders because she wasn't Walter Kelling's little girl any more, and left.

Chapter 3

Cousin Frederick would have made an even plainer old man than Charlie Daventer, Sarah couldn't help thinking as she kissed his wizened cheek. She didn't have to stand on tiptoe to reach it; Frederick wasn't much taller than herself.

His apartment was tiny, too, being no more than an ill-furnished snippet off the end of the kitchen ell of another great barracks much like Emma's. Frederick could have kept the whole house for himself after his parents died if he'd wanted to. Instead, he'd cut off these two little rooms and let the rest to a series of well-heeled tenants. It was commonly supposed the elderly bachelor squirreled away the proceeds along with the rest of his hoard in Swiss banks, safe-deposit boxes, or more likely oatmeal cartons stuffed under his mattress. Only Sarah, Emma, and one or two other Kellings knew Cousin Frederick turned over every penny of his rents and a good deal more besides to a boarding school for handicapped children.

Sarah didn't mind perching on a broken-backed chair under a bare light bulb. She hadn't meant to stay long in any case. She was well aware that Frederick liked to get to bed early in order to save on electricity. Besides, she was tired herself. She admired the new suit, which looked much like any other suit Frederick had ever owned except that it wasn't yet frayed at the cuffs or bagged at the knees, and adjured him to wear it to the show or Aunt Emma would be heartbroken. She listened to the usual reminiscences about her late husband, the usual complaints about his light bills, and the usual diatribe against Cousin Mabel. Then she bade the old curmudgeon a fond good night, for she was warmly attached to Cousin Frederick in spite of everything, and drove the two miles or so back to Aunt Emma's.

She put her car away in the carriage house, being as quiet about it as she could in order not to disturb Mrs. Heatherstone, who had to get up early and make the porridge. The Heatherstones lived in a spacious flat over the vast area that had once been filled with carriages, sleighs, gigs, dogcarts, and horses. Now it held only the big old Buick that Aunt Emma rode in on state occasions with Heatherstone driving, the little red two-seater she scooted around in by herself to luncheons and committee meetings, and the sober Plymouth Mr. and Mrs. Heatherstone used for shopping and to visit their married son at Pelham on their days off. There was plenty of room left over for Sarah.

Back when Uncle Bed's parents were still alive, there'd have been a stable boy to put the car away for her, or at least to hold the big doors open while she drove it inside. Only she wouldn't have been around then, much less driving a car. Anyway, in deference to the march of progress and Heatherstone's advancing years, Mrs. Kelling had installed electric-eye openers that worked with remote-control pushbuttons.

Aunt Emma had no live-in help except the Heatherstones these days. Instead of a red-armed woman bending over a washboard set into a soapstone tub, there were a washer, a dryer, and a mangle in the basement, and a nice lady who came in once a week to run them. Another woman arrived at half-past eight every other morning to tidy the rooms and do the floors. This one preferred to be addressed as a domestic assistant. Aunt Emma said she could be called whatever she pleased provided she didn't forget to mop under the beds, which in fact she never had, so far. The heavy cleaning and yard work were handled by jolly men who came in trucks loaded with rakes and shovels and large appliances, and by college students trying to earn tuition money, all these under the supervision of the Heatherstones. It wasn't much like the old days. In Emma Kelling's opinion, it was far, far better.

Nevertheless, Sarah wouldn't have minded being respectfully attended by a well-muscled stable boy just now. She didn't know why. She wasn't a timid person as a rule, and heaven knew she'd had plenty to be timid about during the past couple of years. Nevertheless, she felt a profound reluctance to walk that fifty feet or so of flagstone path from the well-lighted carriage house to the well-lighted side portico. She hesitated before she pushed the portable control gadget to shut the door behind her, peering all around the garden, trying to catch a glimpse of whatever might be causing her this perturbation.

There was nothing. Emma Kelling was too well aware of the break-ins and muggings that had become so regrettable a common-place occurrence in affluent suburbs. She'd had all the shrubberies within grabbing distance of the walkway cut down ages ago. Nobody was hiding out there, not so much as a skunk or a raccoon or a dog breaking Pleasaunce's strict leash law. There was simply no place to hide. Yet Sarah practically had to get behind herself and shove to start her legs moving along those flagstones.

She'd been given her own latchkey to save Heatherstone's feet. Even as she was turning it in the lock, Sarah was craning over her shoulder to see what so patently wasn't there. She inched the door open barely enough to squeeze her slender frame through, and shut it so fast she caught a fold of her skirt in the crack and had to open it again. Nobody saw her graceless performance. The yard was as vacant now as it had been when she drove in.

Sarah had assumed from the dearth of cars in the drive that Charlie and Ridpath must have left. She was right. She found her aunt sitting alone with Ernestina, humming a snatch from *The Yeomen of the Guard* as a change from philtres and spells, doing a finicky bit of mending on the beaded bag Lady Sangazure was to carry. Nobody in the audience would be able to see whether or not the long-tailed drawstring pouch was missing a few of its beads, but Lady Sangazure would surely never have put up with any hiatus. That was enough for Emma.

When Sarah came in she looked up and smiled. "Well, dear. How's Frederick?"

"Same as always. He told me to give you his best, such as it was."

Sarah repeated as much of Frederick's family gossip as she could remember and reported in detail on the new suit. These things were important to Emma Kelling.

Everything was important to Aunt Emma, she thought. It was this zest for leaping with might and main on everything that came along that kept Beddoes Kelling's widow from ever getting old and dull, kept elderly bachelors dangling on her string for decades, kept elderly husbands hanging around her tea table when they ought to be home at their wives'. Jack Tippleton would have stayed this afternoon even if Gillian Bruges hadn't been handy for ogling.

It wasn't just the old ones, either. Parker Pence openly adored Mrs. Kelling. Guy Mannering was more in love with Emma than with Sarah, though it was silly of him to be either and he'd never have admitted he was. As for the women, not even Cousin

Mabel could think of anything really rotten to say about Emma, though she still hadn't given up trying. Emma Kelling literally did not have an enemy in the world.

Surrounded by all this benign influence, Sarah wondered why she still had the fidgets. She couldn't sit still. Rather than bounce around in a chair, she wandered out to the sun parlor to see if the scenery was dry, though she knew perfectly well it must be, and it was. There'd be no problem when Guy and his crew came to pick it up at the impossible hour he'd set. Presumably somebody would be up to let them in. It might turn out to be Sarah herself. She didn't feel as if she was going to sleep much tonight.

Her aunt was noticing. "Sarah, what's got into you all of a sudden? You're prowling around here like a cat on hot bricks."

"Am I?" Sarah did what Emma would have told her to do twenty years ago: sat down and folded her hands like a good child. "I don't know, Aunt Emma. I'm just edgy. Maybe I'm having one of those psychic premonitions your friend Mrs. Wincley's always going on about. I hope to goodness Max isn't in some kind of trouble."

"Not in Helsinki, surely? Finns always strike one as being so worthy and high-minded. I suppose one could get trampled by a reindeer, or choke on a bone in one's herring salad, but I'm sure Max has sense enough not to.

"Dearie, why don't you nip out to the kitchen and get the tray Mrs. Heatherstone left on the table? It's a vacuum jug of Slepe-o-tite. I always have a cup at night when we're doing a show. One gets so keyed up, you know, and it makes me sleep like a dormouse."

"Slepe-o-tite? Isn't that the stuff you used to make me drink when I stayed with you that time Mama was so sick? I don't believe I've ever tasted it since."

It was odd, Sarah remembered the visit better than she remembered her mother, although Mrs. Walter Kelling had lived another five or six years before she'd at last had to stop protesting that there was nothing much the matter with her. By the time she died, Sarah had been twelve; too old to be shunted off on Aunt Emma, not too young to take over her father's household; at least not by Walter Kelling's reckoning. It was strange to think that if her father hadn't been so fond of gathering wild mushrooms, Sarah might even now be back in that high, narrow, austerely correct house on Pinckney Street, gazing at a lithograph of Ralph Waldo Emerson and trying to think of something cheap but elevating to order for tomorrow's dinner.

She fetched the tray and set it on a taboret in front of her aunt. Emma Kelling filled the two cups from the jug and handed one to Sarah, then took a sip from her own.

"Ugh! Sorry, dear. I'm afraid Mrs. Heatherstone let the milk scorch."

Sarah tasted the stuff and hoped she hadn't made a face. "I'll heat some more milk and make a fresh batch."

"Why bother? It will taste awful no matter what you do. Come now, drink up. It's good for you."

Having been brought up on the same Puritan ethic as her aunt, Sarah gulped it off, except for a half inch or so at the bottom of the cup that she felt entitled to leave for Mr. Manners. Then she kissed Emma good night, carried the jug and cups back to the kitchen, rinsed them out from force of habit, and went upstairs.

At least the stuff seemed to be working. Sarah was already yawning by the time she'd hung up her toothbrush. She fell asleep with the reading light on, and didn't wake up until she heard her aunt and

Heatherstone making a surprising amount of noise out in the upstairs hall.

"That's impossible," Emma was insisting. "It can't be gone. You'd need a truck to carry it off."

"They had a truck, Mrs. Kelling!" Sarah had never heard Heatherstone raise his voice before. "They came at ten minutes past seven this morning. Mrs. Heatherstone let them into the sun parlor because you'd told her to. They loaded the scenery on the truck and drove off."

"But didn't Mrs. Heatherstone watch them?"

"Of course she watched them. She says she stood right there in the doorway and never took her eyes off them for one second. She insists they couldn't have taken anything except what they were supposed to."

"Well, then," said Mrs. Kelling.

By this time Sarah had got on her robe and slippers and run out to join them. "Well then, what? What's the matter?"

"Oh, Sarah!" Emma Kelling couldn't give full voice to the exclamation because she was still wearing her chin strap, but she managed to convey more agitation than Sarah had ever known her to give way to before. "Heatherstone says Ernestina's gone."

"Gone? How can she be? Is he sure?"

Even as she asked, Sarah knew her question was idiotic. How could he not be sure? Nevertheless, she had to run down to the drawing room and see for herself.

The massive baroque frame was still there, hanging over the mantel as always. Inside, however, nothing showed except a rectangle of wall, its gilt tea-paper covering a little brighter than the area outside the frame. Neatly thumbtacked just about where the white dove ought to be perched was a torn-out newspaper headline that read ART THIEVES HOLD PRICELESS MASTERPIECE FOR RANSOM. She was standing on the hearthrug staring up at it when Emma Kelling got to her.

"Sarah, what does that paper mean?"

"I'm afraid it means you're about to get stuck for a lot of money, Aunt Emma."

"Whatever makes them think I'd pay?"

"I can't imagine."

But of course she could. Here was this rich woman in her imposing house. Here was this enormous portrait, not only valuable in itself but presumably freighted with enormous sentimental value for its owner, and her many family connections. It even had a certain historical value, Sarah supposed, for the country, though that was stretching Ernestina somewhat thinner than she'd been in real life.

Emma was noted in the area for her generosity. She might have preferred to handle her philanthropies privately and discreetly like Frederick, but she was too good a showman to underestimate the drawing power of Mrs. Beddoes Kelling's name on a list of donors. She was always throwing her home open for functions in aid of one cause or another. That meant she'd been invaded by any number of strangers along with her friends and acquaintances. Anybody who really knew her ought to have sense enough to realize Emma Kelling could never be pried loose from a cent by threats or coercion. Those who didn't might see only a lone woman with pots of money and what looked like a sure-fire way of getting some away from her.

However could they have got at the Romney, though? Emma had had an elaborate burglar-alarm system installed around the time she'd got rid of her shrubberies. Both she and Heatherstone were punctilious about locking up and making sure all the switches were properly set. Even if they'd both slipped up for once, the security people who were allegedly sitting downtown somewhere monitoring the alarms, not to mention the local police who kept coming around all night in their prowl cars, ought to have known something was wrong.

And why the Romney? Emma Kelling had lots of treasures, including a Monet and a Renoir that Uncle Bed's parents had had the good sense to acquire in Paris back when the Impressionists were going cheap. Neither was large. A thief could have made off with both of them single-handed. They'd have been far more valuable, and infinitely more resalable in case the ransom attempt didn't come off.

So maybe the thief didn't know much of anything about paintings, but had assumed since the Romney was the biggest that it must be the best, and that since Ernestina was a family portrait, she must sit highest in Emma Kelling's regard. Not a very well-informed crook.

Crooks. A theft such as this could not possibly have been a one-man job. Merely to lift the picture down from the wall would have taken the strength of at least two, and perhaps a third up on a ladder to release the chains that held it to the wall from the hooks that held the chains while the others took its weight from below. Then there'd have been the job of unscrewing Ernestina from her frame and hanging the frame back over the mantel.

Why had they bothered to do that? It seemed an unnecessarily time-consuming piece of bravado. Sarah would have thought they'd want to do the job and get away as fast as possible without tacking on any frills. Weren't they afraid of getting caught?

Evidently not, and now that she was getting her wits together, Sarah knew why. That disgusting Slepe-o-tite must have been spiked with something to make sure she and Aunt Emma did indeed get a sound night's sleep. One of the oldest tricks in the book, and she'd swallowed it like a lamb. How would she ever tell Max?

"Aunt Emma," she asked, "how many people know you drink Slepe-o-tite every night when you're doing a show?"

"Sarah dear, this is hardly the time for irrelevancies."

"This isn't one. Don't you recall how drowsy you were last night when you went upstairs?"

"Was I?"

"You were yawning your head off. So was I, even though you'd been saying just a little while before what a fidget I was in, which I was. That's why you gave me a cup of your Slepe-o-tite. And we both thought it tasted worse than usual. You said Mrs. Heatherstone must have scorched the milk, but can you actually imagine her doing such a thing? And I don't know how that stuff is supposed to work, but I was out like a light from the moment I hit the pillow until you and Heatherstone woke me just now."

"Come to think of it, so was I, and that's not usual at my time of life. Heatherstone, did you have any trouble waking me?"

"I did, Mrs. Kelling. It may interest you to know that Mrs. Heatherstone also had a hard time waking me. Furthermore, she was complaining that she herself had overslept. She said she was up barely in time to let in those young fellows who came after the scenery, and you know that's not like her."

"She still goes to bed at half-past nine?" Sarah asked him.

"Regular as clockwork," Heatherstone assured her. "Me having to be up later, she lets me sleep on till breakfast time, then rings me on the house phone. She claims she had to let it ring and ring this morning till she'd begun to wonder if something had happened to me before I answered."

"Did you and she drink Slepe-o-tite last night too?"

"We did. Mrs. Heatherstone fixed a jug for us when

she did Mrs. Kelling's, and carried it across with her when she quit for the night."

"Did she do that last thing before she went, or would the jugs have been left to sit for a while?" Sarah asked him.

"Seems to me she always scalds the milk while she's still working around the stove, which means she'd mix the Slepe-o-tite as soon as it's hot. That way she doesn't wind up with an extra pan to wash after everything else is redded up. Mrs. Heatherstone's a great one for making her head save her hands, you know."

"There you are, Sarah," said Emma Kelling. "We've all been doped like a stableful of race horses. I daresay I shall find it an interesting experience if I ever manage to get rid of this headache. Heatherstone, would your wife have any undrugged coffee available?"

"I hope so, ma'am. I just drank some of it myself."

"You don't feel sleepy?"

"Just a bit logy, as you might say."

"Then bring us some in the boudoir. Come along, Sarah. We'd better go upstairs and make ourselves presentable before any more burglars pop in."

"Mrs. Kelling," said Heatherstone, "should I call the police before I bring the coffee, or would you rather I waited till after?"

"Don't you dare call them at all. I don't want a word of this breathed to anybody till I've had time to think about it. Please tell Mrs. Heatherstone I said so. Not that she would, of course," Emma added hastily, for this was no time to get the cook's back up. "Sarah, I suggest you take a cold shower to wake you up, and get dressed as quickly as you can. Then come to the boudoir. We need to talk."

Chapter 4

They'd need to do more than talk, but Sarah could see why her aunt might hesitate about calling in the police. Aside from the Heatherstones, assuming a pair of faithful retainers well into their sixties were physically able, much less criminally inclined to juggle that enormous painting around, the likeliest suspects were Emma Kelling and Sarah Bittersohn.

It wouldn't be much good arguing to even a reasonably astute patrolman that Emma Kelling could not possibly have stolen her own Romney. A sizable percentage of Max Bittersohn's large yearly income was derived from insurance companies whose clients had staged burglaries to collect the premiums.

Even if Emma Kelling could prove she didn't need any more money, she'd have a hard time persuading the authorities that she hadn't thought it might be nice to get some anyway. Even if she got her minister, the Town Counsel, and every single member of all her committees to swear to her strict moral probity, there'd still be those who doubted. Too many people knew too much about Emma Kelling's propensity to take a shot at whatever was going.

Emma scorned the vulgarly exhibitionistic and the blatantly spectacular, but not many of the Fairy Queens who'd played *Iolanthe* since its premiere on November 5, 1882, had been swung down from the flies in a bosun's chair wearing blown-up canvas water wings instead of the usual gauzy alar appurtenances. It was not so much the bustle she'd be wearing as the high-wheeled bicycle she planned to ride up to Sir Marmaduke's mansion that would tend to set Mrs. Kelling apart from other Lady Sanga-zures.

Emma had been up in a balloon and down in a bathysphere. After she had spearheaded a drive to buy Pleasaunce a new fire engine, she'd insisted on taking the vast machine for a trial run herself and personally climbed the eighty-foot extension ladder all the way to the top before she turned over the check to pay for it, not to gain publicity but simply to make sure the town was getting its money's worth. Nobody who knew her could ever suspect Emma Kelling of stealing her own painting for an ignoble purpose, but neither would they be able to envision her hanging back if she should happen to think of a noble one.

Trying to get her thoughts straight, Sarah stayed under the shower longer than she'd meant to. By the time she'd got her clothes on and waded through the deep golden plush of the hall carpet to her aunt's blue and cream boudoir, she found Emma minus her chin strap and cold cream, dressed for action in one of the self-effacing beige and gray outfits she affected. For camouflage, Cousin Frederick said. Her face was discreetly made up and her pale blond hair in impeccable order.

Sarah knew how that elaborate coiffure had been managed so quickly. Emma had five more just like it, all lined up on wig blocks in her closet. She really was a marvelous organizer. If Emma Kelling ever did take a notion to perpetrate the perfect crime— but that was nonsense. She and Sarah had both drunk from the same jug. Sarah herself had fetched the tray and poured out the drink. There was no way on earth the drug could have been slipped into her cup, assuming Aunt Emma would ever dream of doing such a thing.

She could have been drugged some other way, of course. Whatever had made the Slepe-o-tite taste so particularly awful last night might in fact have been only scorched milk, or something equally innocent. The sedative could have been slipped into her bed-side carafe, or sprayed on her toothbrush. Or injected by a snake trained to slither into her room via the hole in the floor where the radiator pipes came up and give her an only mildly venomous bite. Sarah sat down on one of the blue velvet slipper chairs and took the cup of coffee her aunt had poured out for her.

"You know, Sarah," said Mrs. Kelling, "I've been thinking."

"As well you might," Sarah replied when her aunt didn't say any more. "Would you care to tell me what about?"

"It's just that I can't for the life of me see how anybody got at Ernestina. Heatherstone says he went around and checked all the locks before he came to tell me she was gone. He swears there's no sign of a break-in anywhere."

"The burglar alarm must have been off, though," Sarah pointed out. "Mrs. Heatherstone would have had to throw the switch before she let in Guy and his crew to get the scenery, wouldn't she? Unless it was off already."

"If it was, I can't think why she hasn't said. Unless Heatherstone never thought to ask her."

Emma Kelling jotted a reminder in the brand-new blue memo book she had lying in front of her on a slim-legged gilt and cream writing desk. Emma's little blue notebooks were a legend around Plea-saunce. She always started a fresh book for any proj-ect she embarked on. A stack of crisp new ones were kept on hand in her desk, and a pile of used ones

were heaped up in her great-grandmother's wedding
chest that sat just outside the boudoir door, each of
them dog-eared from being carried around, filled with
memoranda written in her clear, square hand, each
item meticulously checked off as she'd dealt with it.
How like Emma, to start a notebook for Ernestina.
Sarah hoped she wouldn't have to put in many en-
tries.

"Well, naturally we can rule out the Heatherstones," Sarah said. "Nevertheless, it does seem as
if this had to be something in the nature of an inside
job. There's that business of the Slepe-o-tite, for instance. You still haven't told me how many people
know you take it."

"Oh. Well, I suppose quite a few. People get keyed
up, you know, and come to me complaining that they
haven't been getting their sleep because they're worried about coming down with a cold or fluffing their
lines or whatever. So I tell them about Aunt Emma's
own special soothing syrup. I even have Mrs. Heatherstone keep a few extra jars on hand so I can dole
them out to extreme cases."

"Would these people know the Heatherstones
drink Slepe-o-tite, too?"

Emma shrugged. "I shouldn't be surprised. I take
a certain amount of teasing about my old-fashioned
patent remedies, you know. People tell me it's all in
the mind, and ask Heatherstone if the stuff really
works or if I'm having pipe dreams. I suppose he
assures them that he knows it does because he and
his wife take it, too. You know Heatherstone, he's
not precisely your stiff-upper-lip British butler. In
the first place, he's no more British than you or I.
His people came from Connecticut. And he's certainly no mere butler, more like a resident guardian
angel. I couldn't possibly manage without the Heatherstones, and that's one reason I don't want to call
the police. Rather than have them accused of pinch-

ing the Romney, I'd sooner let them keep it, supposing they had. But they didn't, I'm positive. Why should they?"

"I can't imagine. Medical bills?"

"Never. I pay their medical insurance myself. Furthermore, they're both old enough to qualify for Medicare if they needed it, which they don't. As for the son, he has a marvelous job and his whole family's on some unbelievably comprehensive master plan. They even get their teeth fixed without having to pay."

Sarah had no desire to play devil's advocate, but she supposed they might as well settle the point once and for all. "Maybe one of the grandchildren's in a jam."

"They don't get into jams. They're all Eagle Scouts and win scholarships to the most prestigious schools. Sarah dear, you simply must not waste your time suspecting the Heatherstones."

"I wasn't. I was just clearing the air. Then that leaves your two housecleaners and the members of the cast."

"Yes, I'm afraid it does," Emma agreed. "That's the other reason why I can't call the police. They're terribly efficient around here. They'd probably find the culprit right away, and then where would I be? I'm sure it's not Mrs. Knowles or Mrs. DeWitt. They've been with me for years and they'd know enough to steal something more portable than Ernestina if they were going to steal anything at all, which they never have so far, so why should they take a notion to do it now? So that leaves the cast, and can't you just see the headlines? KIND AND REVEREND RECTOR TURNS ART THIEF. What good would that kind of publicity do us, and whom could we get to fill his part? I can't imagine the police would let him perform, can you?"

"Aunt Emma, do you really think it was Sebastian Frostedd who kidnapped Ernestina?"

"Sebastian? Oh, Sarah, don't take me seriously. I was only thinking what an interesting headline he'd make. More coffee?"

"Please. You did mean Sebastian, though, didn't you?"

Emma sighed. "Darling, I simply don't know. I will admit Bed used to say it wasn't safe to open your mouth around Sebastian Frostedd because he'd pick the fillings right out of your teeth if he got a chance. I'm surprised Dolph hasn't given you an earful."

"Oh, he has. Dolph claims Sebastian swiped his own mother's ukulele when he was ten, and pawned it so he'd have money to spend on liquor and women when he got old enough, but you know Dolph. He says Sebastian's never earned an honest dollar in his life. Neither has Dolph, but then Dolph's never earned a crooked one, either. Those Senior Citizens' Recycling Centers he and Mary have started pay surprisingly well, but it's the recyclers who earn the money, and it all goes straight back to them."

"Imagine Dolph Kelling a junkman." Despite her own perturbation, Emma managed to laugh. "I'm so glad he's found his niche at last. I don't know about the ukulele, but after some of the tales Bed used to tell, I'd believe just about anything. All of which doesn't alter the fact that Sebastian makes a superb Dr. Daly and there's no way we can get along without him."

"Aunt Emma, does *The Sorcerer* actually mean more to you than the Romney?"

"At the moment, yes, to be quite frank with you. I've never thought of Ernestina as mine. She's just one more of the heirlooms Bed and I somehow wound up holding in trust for the Kelling family. Naturally I'd hate to feel I'd fallen down on the job Bed left me to do, but personally I'm going to feel a thousand percent worse if this show flops. I'm sorry if I've shocked you, but that's the way it is. You know, Sarah, I'm really too old to be doing this again. I've no voice left and precious little wind. I've made up my mind that Lady Sangazure's the last role I'll ever do, but I'm still vain enough to want to go out in a blaze of glory."

Emma took a sip of her coffee. "Do try to see my point of view, Sarah. The show will be over three days from now. That's not long to wait. Anyway, if Ernestina's actually being held for ransom, we have a little time, I should think. It's going to take whoever stole her a while to cut out all those letters from the newspaper and stick the ransom note together, shouldn't you think? Isn't that the accepted procedure?"

"Nowadays I believe they simply telephone."

"Then in that case we have absolutely nothing to worry about. They won't be able to get a call through because the line will be busy right up till curtain time. It always is. What I'm getting at, darling, is that nothing dreadful's going to happen to Ernestina until I've been given a chance to pay the ransom and I can't realistically be expected to do that in the wink of an eyelash, can I? So we simply stall the thieves along until I've sung my swan song, then we call the police and get everything straightened out. You see?"

Sarah didn't see at all, but she never got a chance to say so. The gilt and ivory French phone on her aunt's *poudrière* was already ringing. Somebody was being terribly sorry to bother Emma so early but she simply had to know what was happening about the baskets for the auditorium because somebody else had this minute called to say she'd fallen and wrenched her shoulder so she couldn't possibly.

"What a dreadful shame. No, it's quite all right. My niece is going to take care of them. Yes, the scenery's all finished and delivered. Not a thing in the world to fret yourself about. Thank you for calling."

Emma put the receiver back on its cradle. "That woman hasn't the common sense of a good-sized rabbit. But she'll work her head off for you so long as you don't expect her to think with it. You will get at those baskets right after breakfast, won't you? I hate to slave-drive, but I want this performance to be perfect in every way. You do understand, don't you? Now come along. Mrs. Heatherstone must be wondering what's kept us."

Breakfast at Emma Kelling's was porridge, eggs, bacon, muffins, toast, and marmalade. Sarah ate it all, in a sort of sinking-of-the-*Titanic* mood. Anyway, lunch would probably be salad and yogurt. Her aunt was wont to take spasms of dieting in the middle of the day, provided she didn't have a luncheon engagement, as she so often did. In the midst of buttering a piece of muffin, Sarah had a thought.

"Aunt Emma, didn't you say you were having the whole cast over here tonight, chorus, orchestra, and all, for supper and a pre-dress rehearsal?"

"That's right. We'd hoped to have it in the auditorium, but they're booked for a dance recital or some ridiculous thing."

"Then what about the Romney? People will notice that great, gaping hole inside the frame and ask questions."

"Oh dear, so they will. I hadn't thought of that. I'll have to pretend I've sent it away to be cleaned."

"But you've already told Ridpath Wale you didn't want to bother until after the show."

"Then I'll tell him I changed my mind."

"He won't believe you. When did you ever? Anyway, how could you have made the arrangements on such short notice? Last night you said you didn't even know whom to call."

Sarah added a dollop of marmalade to her muffin

and finished it off. "I'll tell you what," she said when she could talk again, "I could slap off a comic portrait of you as Lady Sangazure on a piece of the leftover scenery canvas and stick that into the frame. The cast will think it's just part of the fun."

"Darling, that would be magnificent! But can you?"

"I don't know, but I can try. It doesn't have to be good, you know."

"I didn't mean that kind of 'can you,' I meant will you have time? There are all those baskets to be done."

"What about your garden club? Couldn't you get some of them to cut your greens?"

"Good heavens, it's high time I was put out to pasture. The garden club never crossed my mind. I'll just make a couple of phone calls."

Emma Kelling was off and running again. Sarah picked up some of the breakfast dishes and carried them out to the kitchen.

"Why, Sarah, you didn't have to do that," Mrs. Heatherstone fussed. "Here, set them on the drainboard. I'll get the rest."

"This was just an excuse to talk to you." Sarah got rid of her load. "Mrs. Heatherstone, I'm sure your husband must have told you what we think happened last night."

"About us all drinking the poisoned Slepe-o-tite? I can't believe it."

"It can't have been poisoned, just loaded with sleeping pills or something of that sort. Didn't it taste strange to you when you drank it?"

"No worse than usual. I hate Slepe-o-tite, if you want the truth."

"Then why do you drink it?"

The cook shrugged. "Because it's good for me, I suppose. Mrs. Kelling says so, anyway. Come to think of it, I wouldn't have tasted the Slepe-o-tite much last night anyway. Mr. Frostedd brought me a lovely

box of those chocolate-covered liqueur cherries I'm
so fond of, and I'd been eating a few of them while
I was reading the paper before I went to bed. Not
that I need 'em, the Lord knows," she sighed, smooth-
ing her apron over her ample frontage. "But anyway,
I remember taking one more just before I drank the
Slepe-o-tite, figuring the maraschino would take the
taste out of my mouth. I guess likely it did, all right."

"That's interesting. Would your husband have
eaten some, too, do you suppose?"

"Oh yes, I expect so. Mr. Heatherstone's not one
for snacking between meals as a rule, but he does
enjoy a little bite of something sweet before bed-
time."

"I see," said Sarah, who had a fairly good idea
that she did. "When did Mr. Frostedd give you the
cherries?"

"Yesterday afternoon, right after he got here, I
suppose it must have been. He came out to the kitchen
and told me how much he appreciated all the nice
teas and dinners he'd been getting here since we
started working on the show. He knew how much
extra work it must be making for me, and he just
wanted to do a little something to show his appre-
ciation."

"How thoughtful of him. Is Mr. Frostedd in the
habit of bringing you presents?"

"Well, no, I can't say as he is. He'll come out here
and pass the time of day once in a while when the
spirit moves him, but he doesn't usually bring me
anything. He's more apt to help himself to some of
whatever happens to be on the table, if you want the
truth. Not that I mind, and not that Mrs. Kelling
would ever begrudge a bite to a living soul. You know
how open-handed she is."

"Oh no, she wouldn't mind," Sarah assured her.
"Now, Mrs. Heatherstone, I don't want to put ideas
into your head that aren't there already, but I wonder

if you could just tell me where those two thermos jugs were when Mr. Frostedd came into the kitchen."

"Sarah Kelling, you're not trying to tell me a nice man like him would do a thing like that?"

Sarah knew that scolding tone of old. For a fleeting moment she wondered if she was about to be sent to her room. "I'm not trying to tell you anything, Mrs. Heatherstone," she pleaded. "I just want to know. Mr. Frostedd has a habit of teasing my aunt about her Slepe-o-tite, she says. I was thinking he might have made some joke to you about it."

"Oh, now I get what you're driving at, though I must say I don't see what's so funny about Slepe-o-tite. Let's see, now. No, I hadn't put the jugs out yet. They must still have been in the butler's pantry."

"Whereabouts in the butler's pantry?"

"Sitting on the counter above that long cabinet where we store the larger serving pieces. Normally I'd set them down inside, but my back's been bothering me so lately that anything I know I'm likely to want again right away, I just leave on top. Saves me having to stoop so much."

Sarah made the appropriate noises about Mrs. Heatherstone's back. She was picturing the butler's pantry, not really a separate room in this house but a rather narrow passage lined on both sides with glass-fronted china cabinets and lockable silver drawers, separated from both the kitchen and the dining room by swinging doors. She'd just come through there herself. Sebastian would have done the same to reach the kitchen, unless he'd gone around and come through from the back of the house, which would have been absurd. So he'd have had plenty of time alone with the jugs both coming and going.

"Thermos jugs tend to scare me a little," she remarked. "I always think I have to scald them out with hot water before I put in anything hot, for fear of cracking the glass liner."

"You always were an old-fashioned child, Sarah. That might have been true years back, before they got this tempered glass, or whatever they call it, but I don't think it makes any difference these days. Though I must say I do it myself, often as not."

"Did you rinse out the jugs last night?"

Mrs. Heatherstone had to stop and think. Then she shook her head. "I can't for the life of me remember. I might have and I mightn't, that's the best I can tell you. The jugs were washed clean yesterday morning, I do know that. I'm not one to leave dirty dishes sitting around."

"I know you're not." This wasn't helping a bit. "Would you happen to recall whether any other member of the cast came into the kitchen last night?"

"Nope. I can swear to that easily enough. Mind you, I'm not saying one of them couldn't have snuck into the pantry and dropped something into those jugs, if that's what you're driving at. They'd have had to be pretty nippy about it, though. Mr. Heatherstone was back and forth a lot, serving the tea and setting the table and getting ice for the drinks and whatnot. He never got a chance to sit down to his own dinner till after he'd taken the coffee into the drawing room. Not that he minds, as I'm sure I don't have to tell you. He always has an early tea and a little rest, knowing Mrs. Kelling as we do, so we're ready for anything by the time she tells us she's got company coming unexpected."

"So in fact it would have been—what? About half-past eight before the coast was clear for somebody to get into the pantry undisturbed?"

"Closer to nine, I should say. But by then I'd have had the jugs in the kitchen with me. I remember putting the milk on to heat in the double boiler and going in to get the jugs, and hearing you all talking around the dinner table. Mrs. Kelling was saying she'd have the buffet set out in the sun parlor by the time people began arriving for the rehearsal. That was news to me. I'd assumed she'd want Mr. Heatherstone to serve drinks and hors d'oeuvres in the drawing room first as usual, which would have given me extra time to be setting the food out in the dining room. They often want the sun parlor clear for rehearsing the dance numbers, you see, because the tiled floor out there's easier to skip around on than the drawing-room carpets."

"Yes, I see."

"I wouldn't want you to think I make a practice of eavesdropping, Sarah, but this was my business as much as anybody's, so I stayed there till I'd made sure what the plans were. Then I had to run back and grab the milk off the stove before it came up to the boil, and let the Slepe-o-tite cool down a little before I poured it into the jugs. Mrs. Kelling hates to scald her tongue."

So much for Aunt Emma's scorched-milk theory.

"After you'd finished and Mr. Heatherstone had taken the coffee into the drawing room, he and I sat down here at the kitchen table and had a bite of dinner ourselves, as I told you. Then we took care of the dishes together, and I took our jug of Slepe-o-tite and the box of cherries I mentioned and went along to our place."

Then there had been a short interval, though perhaps only a couple of minutes, when somebody could have ducked into the kitchen and dropped a sedative into the pan of milk that was heating on the stove. Who, for instance? Everybody but Charlie Daventer and Ridpath Wale had left. Sarah knew perfectly well neither of them had got up till Emma gave the signal, and that they'd all four gone back to the drawing room together. Soon after that, however, she herself had gone off to Cousin Frederick's.

And what if she had? By that time the Heather-

stones must have been eating their own belated dinner with the filled jugs sitting right under their noses.
Then Mrs. Heatherstone had taken one of them and
gone home. It made no sense whatever, as far as she
could see, to imagine the jugs could have been tampered with after that. The doping must have been
done while they were sitting in the butler's pantry.

"Unless somebody sneaked in the back door," she
said aloud.

Mrs. Heatherstone snorted. "That's crazy, Sarah
Kelling, if you don't mind me saying so. That back
door's always locked, and it stays locked or I don't
stay in this kitchen. I said so to Mrs. Kelling as soon
as I heard about what happened to that cook of the
Terwilligers', and she agrees with me one hundred
percent."

"Well, of course. I was only wondering. Now, about
those scenery flats that were picked up this morning.
Mr. Heatherstone says you stood right there and
watched the men carry them out."

"I did, not that they were what I'd call men. It
was just that Mannering boy and a couple of his
friends. One was Skip and the other was Chill. I
suppose they must have real names, but I never heard
'em. Anyway, they took out the big square pieces
first, that make up the house, you know, and then
the other ones that have the bushes painted on them.
I eyed them like a hawk the whole time because I
was afraid they'd scar the nice, clean woodwork Mrs.
Kelling just had repainted, and I'm willing to swear
that was all they took. Mr. Heatherstone asked me
if maybe the painting could have got carried out with
the scenery. I told him I didn't see how, though I
could see where he got the idea, all of them being
just canvas stretched over a framework."

"Perhaps he meant they might have hidden it between two of the other flats."

"Not unless they were magicians, they didn't. Guy

was scared stiff they'd scratch up the artwork, as he called it, and I was worried for fear they'd get smart and poke a hole in one of the windows, let alone mess up the paint, so we made sure each piece was handled separately. Furthermore, they'd have had to be taking an awful chance, pulling a stunt like that in broad daylight."

Not really, Sarah thought, if Guy had taken the forethought to disguise Ernestina with a skin of new canvas painted to look like part of Sir Marmaduke's mansion when she was taken out of the frame and stacked her with the rest of the flats. Theoretically, Guy could even have laid down a fresh ground and painted scenery right on top of the old canvas, but Sarah didn't think Guy would have had enough time or skill to manage that, even if he'd had all night to work on the project.

Assuming for the sake of argument that Guy and his cronies had stolen Ernestina and managed to get her out of the house right under Mrs. Heatherstone's nose, they'd have had to be awfully harebrained to truck her all the way to the auditorium. Guy must know Emma Kelling well enough by now to realize she was apt as not to swoop down for a pre-breakfast ride on her high-wheeled bicycle to make sure they'd got the scenery delivered safely, and that she'd know merely by the dimensions if one flat was actually her Romney.

Sarah supposed it wouldn't hurt to go and take a look, but how could she? There was that fake Romney to be painted and all those baskets of greenery to be got ready before the cast started to arrive at half-past five this afternoon. Aunt Emma would be going down there soon; let her take a tape measure along and see what she might find. Nothing but scenery, was Sarah's guess. As for herself, she must get to work. What a shame Cousin Brooks wasn't around

to build her a stretcher and help stretch the canvas.
She herself was no good at that sort of thing.

Come to think of it, Cousin Frederick was. He'd
taught himself to do all sorts of odd jobs for his tenants, in order to get out of paying a handyman. Surely
he could nail four pieces of wood together and tack
a piece of canvas over the middle. She wouldn't have
to tell him why it was needed, just that it was one
of Aunt Emma's bright ideas. She ran to the phone.

Chapter 5

Frederick groused a bit, but he came. By the time he'd assembled the stretcher, Sarah had completed a sketch of her aunt on a huge piece of brown wrapping paper, throwing in as much detail as she could recall from the Romney and adding a few touches of her own. Her birdbath was all right, but the dove turned out to look more like a Boston Common pigeon. She wasn't going to worry about that. This was merely another piece of scenery. All that counted was the general effect.

Together, she and Frederick stretched the canvas, tugging at opposite sides of the crude frame, whanging in staples and tugging some more. Considering that this was a maiden effort for both of them, they didn't do too badly. Sarah transferred her drawing to the canvas, corrected it here and there, and lined up her paints. By lunchtime she'd slapped on a vaguely gardenish background and got the figure blocked in. She knocked off gratefully for a quick bite and sup, then went back to work. By three o'clock she'd produced a reasonably credible likeness of Emma Kelling in her purple bustle, complete with roses and lorgnette. The lorgnette was a detail Romney hadn't happened to think of. Nor, for a wonder, had Emma, but Sarah put one in anyway.

Then came the problem of getting Lady Sangazure into Ernestina's frame. That took the combined efforts of Sarah, Frederick, Emma, and the Heather-

stones, none of them any great shakes as weight
lifters, but the consensus was that the effect was
worth the effort. "And now, Sarah," said Emma Kelling, "the baskets."

The ladies from the garden club had known far
better than Sarah how much greenery those big baskets were going to swallow. They'd stacked the flag-
stoned flower room full of branches, along with plastic
buckets of tulips and daffodils that were being, Sarah
gathered, conditioned.

One kind soul had even stayed to help. So, for a
wonder, did Cousin Frederick. The three of them
filled dishpans with bricks of Oasis, taped chicken
wire over this unlikely assemblage, forced the filled
pans down inside the baskets, and began sticking
the greens through the holes in the wire, into the
Oasis. First, it turned out, stems had to be bashed
to let the water up through. This was all news to
Frederick, but he willingly elected himself chief
basher so that Sarah and her new mentor, called Peg,
could work off their aesthetic urges on the baskets.

Gradually the arrangements took shape. At four
o'clock Heatherstone brought them cups of tea. At
five, Peg had to go and pick up her daughter from
dancing class. At half-past, they began to hear cast
and orchestra members arriving. At a quarter to six,
Sarah and Frederick thrust the last well-bashed
branches into the baskets and called it quits.

There was to be no dressing for dinner tonight
since there was no dinner, only the buffet set out in
the sun parlor so that performers could help themselves as they wished during lulls in the rehearsal.
Sarah and her elderly cousin merely washed off the
pitch and joined the throng. That was when they
heard about Charlie Daventer.

"You mean to say you didn't know?" That was
Sebastian Frostedd, spreading the news. He had a
rather dark whiskey and soda in his hand, Sarah

noticed. "The cleaning woman found Charlie this morning, in his pajamas. Evidently he'd got up in the night, slipped on the bath mat, and hit his head on the edge of the tub."

"My God, you don't mean Charlie's dead?" Frederick stared at Sebastian for a second or two, then went and got himself an even darker drink.

Ridpath Wale came up beside Sebastian, shaking his head and making the right noises. "When you think we were all here together just twenty-four hours ago, having a fine time. Charlie looked great then. Didn't you think so, Sarah?"

Yes, Sarah had thought so.

Ridpath finished his drink and slammed the empty glass down on the buffet table. "Well, the show must go on. Charlie wouldn't have wanted us to stand around with long faces. Eat, drink, and be gay. Banish all worry and sorrow. Laugh gaily today, weep (if you're sorry) tomorrow."

His full baritone rose easily above the conversation. Others picked up the chorus. The show was going on. Only Emma Kelling was not singing.

"That's all very well," she snapped, "but what are we going to do for a Notary? Two nights before opening, and no time to rehearse. And Charlie gone." She faltered, then threw up her head somewhat in the manner of Boadicea facing the Roman legions. "Frederick, you'll have to take Charlie's part."

"Me?" Her cousin choked on his drink. "Emma, you're out of your mind."

"I am no such thing. You'll manage splendidly. By the way, Frederick Kelling, I hope you haven't forgotten who got you off the hook that time you got drunk on bathtub gin and wound up engaged to Cousin Mabel."

"For God's sake, Emma! That was in June of 1929."

"It was 1928. And the statute of limitations hasn't run out as far as I'm concerned. Frederick, you owe

me. Furthermore, if you don't come across, I'll tell
Mabel precisely how the disengagement was ef-
fected."

"Emma, you wouldn't."

"Frederick, I would. I'm a desperate woman."

She glared him down. At last Frederick sighed,
shrugged, took a mighty swig from his glass, and
muttered, "All right, Emma. What do I have to do?"

"Not a great deal, actually. You only have a few
lines, and we can write them down on a habeas cor-
pus or something for you to carry around with you.
Come along, everybody. Finish your suppers and let's
get started."

Thus ended the period of mourning. Emma was
clearly heartsick over losing her devoted swain of
more than half a century, but she was a trouper first
and last. As for the others, Sarah suspected most of
them were simply relieved. One person's tragedy, she
knew from too much experience, tends to be another's
social embarrassment. The younger members of the
cast had barely known Charlie Daventer, since he'd
had to miss so many rehearsals. The older ones were
perhaps finding his sudden death too uncomfortable
a reminder that such things could happen to anybody, any time, but were more likely to happen to
people in their age bracket.

Whatever their motivations, they all acted glad
of the excuse to tuck Charlie's demise under the carpet for the time being. Telling each other they'd be
working off the calories, they helped themselves
recklessly from the buffet and the bar. Talk grew
louder, more excited. Members of the chorus gathered to practice their footwork on the smooth tile
floor. Featured performers made polite suggestions
to their fellows about not hogging the footlights. The
orchestra members, seasoned veterans that they
were, concentrated on the refreshments.

Sarah concentrated on the company. Her aunt had

hissed to her, "Make them eat. Don't let anybody get tight, for goodness' sake," so she darted around to trouble spots with plates of sandwiches and kept a wary eye on the bar. As soon as she could decently assume they'd had enough, she started herding the players into the drawing room.

The first to allow herself to be herded was Martha Tippleton, their Dame Partlett. Hers is a small supporting role, like the Notary's, but she does carry the distinction of having the first spoken lines in the show. Martha appeared to be finding this a ponderous responsibility, but then Martha often looked to be oppressed by one thing or another. Living with Jack Tippleton, Sarah thought, she naturally would.

Martha must have been absolutely stunning when she was young. She was still lovely in a middle-aged way, with huge, sad gray eyes in a pale, thin-boned face, and tiny hands that tended to flutter. She was not, perhaps, the ideal type for a pew opener, but Emma had determined her friend was not to be shunted into the chorus and there was no other part for a woman her age except Lady Sangazure. Martha hadn't the physique or the voice for that robust role, even if Emma could have borne to step aside and let her take a whack at it.

What was going to happen to the Pirates of Pleasaunce once their *prima donna assoluta* hung up her bustle? Sarah had a feeling that without Emma thundering across the boards, the company would fall apart almost at once. This might not be only Emma's swan song, but the whole company's. Just now, it didn't seem so unreasonable that Emma chose to put her production before her stolen portrait.

At least Ernestina's absence wasn't causing an uncomfortable stir. Sarah's life-sized caricature of Lady Sangazure had been noticed and the air was full of "Too clever for words" and an "Utterly killing" that Sarah could have done nicely without now that she'd been presented with the uncomfortable coincidence of Charlie Daventer's death on the same night his liege lady's Romney disappeared. She could also have dispensed with Ridpath Wale's comment about Emma's having changed her mind rather suddenly, hadn't she?

"What about?" Sarah asked him, all innocence.

"About having the Romney cleaned. She told us last night she wasn't going to bother until after the show."

"Who said she's bothering? This is just a joke Frederick and I cooked up with the Heatherstones' help. I'd got so carried away with scene painting that I couldn't stop. Do put on *Ruddigore* next year so I can do the family portraits. You'd be divine as Sir Ruthven Murgatroyd. Whatever is Gillian Bruges doing over there? Oughtn't she to be rehearsing with Cousin Frederick? Excuse me."

Gillian wasn't doing anything out of the way, but that was beside the point. Sarah only wanted to escape before Ridpath Wale asked her anything more about Ernestina. She didn't know if he was just making conversation, or fishing to see what line the household was taking over a theft he wasn't supposed to know anything about. She did know this was no time to explode another bombshell among the cast. Charlie's death had already aggravated their preopening jitters. Dame Partlett was in a real state, from the look of her. Aline kept having fits of the giggles that sounded altogether too much like hysterics. Sir Marmaduke seemed to be hunting an excuse to throw a temperament.

Others were nervy, too, but the Tippletons were the worst. It must be more than Charlie Daventer that was bothering them. A full-scale family row just before they left home was a likely explanation. Sarah hoped they weren't going to start it up again here. She was wondering how she might safely pour some oil on the waters when, to her amazement, Cousin Frederick hurled himself into the breach.

"Come here, Martha. It appears you get stuck with me at the end, so you may as well get used to me now. Show me what I'm supposed to do."

"I'd love to, Fred, but not just yet. I'm on as soon as the chorus finishes the opening number. Stand by and give me moral support. You don't appear till almost the end of the act."

Frederick took Martha's arm and held it till she had to participate in the short recitative that leads to her stage daughter's first solo. Sarah noted with amusement that Jack Tippleton tried to get close to Gillian and that Emma headed him off, backing him into a corner with Peter and Sebastian to await their upcoming cue.

The moral support Martha was getting from Frederick must be doing the trick. She was more relaxed now, projecting motherly concern in a sweet, true alto. Then Gillian began her mournful confession of unrequited adoration. Sarah could have smacked her for keeping her eyes fixed on Jack Tippleton instead of the kind and reverend rector as she lamented that his love alone could give her aching heart release. Nevertheless, Sarah had to admit Aunt Emma had been lucky to get so good a voice.

Gillian knew how to project to an audience, too. She ought to, Sarah thought nastily, she practiced on everybody who came handy. She was into her second stanza now, and giving young Parker Pence the treatment. Ridpath Wale, whom Sarah had hoped she'd shaken, was still there and much amused.

"Can't she make up her mind which one she's after?" he muttered.

"Neither," Sarah murmured back. "She's only trying to make you jealous."

Maybe she was. Ridpath was no ladykiller like Jack but he was personable enough, some years younger, and a good deal richer according to Dolph Kelling, who always knew these things. Ridpath was also, at the moment, single. If Gillian simply wanted a man, why didn't she look where the picking was better?

Unless she didn't really want one at all. Perhaps all she cared for was the thrill of the chase. As did Jack Tippleton, according to Aunt Emma and a number of disgruntled Tessas and Gianettas. Well, good luck to them both.

Gillian finished her number and got her applause. Martha went back to stand beside Frederick, who reached over to pat her shoulder and let his hand rest there. Sarah wished Jack Tippleton would notice, but he was still eying Gillian like a cat after a canary. He moved again to escape, but Emma forestalled him. Dr. Daly was beginning his solo.

"Time was when love and I were well acquainted. Time was when we walked ever hand in hand."

Sarah wasn't buying that. She doubted that Sebastian Frostedd had ever given two hoots and a holler for anybody except himself. As for his having been a saintly youth with worldly thoughts untainted, one could but smile and shrug. Sebastian did project the aura of the pulpit to perfection, though, his rubicund face bland and gentle in the warm glow from Emma Kelling's handsome brass and crystal girandoles.

Whatever his own feelings or lack of them, one could credit the possibility that time had been when ladies of the noblest station, forsaking even military men, could have gazed upon him rapt in adoration. A few might even be doing so now, though Sarah couldn't see any indication of it. Any woman would have to be a fool to take Sebastian Frostedd seriously, but at least he didn't have a wife and daughter in tow, and he'd probably be more fun on a date than Jack Tippleton.

Chacun à son gout. Here came Sir Marmaduke, out of his corner at last with the brave Alexis in tow. There went Dr. Daly to offer them his best, his very best congratulations. Sarah decided the show could go on without her.

She wandered back out to the sun parlor and began checking the window fastenings. They were good, heavy, competent solid brass locks, showing no sign of having been tampered with. Sarah inspected them all nevertheless, heard the chorus shrieking that with heart and with voice they were welcoming this meeting, and refrained from going back into the drawing room. She herself wouldn't welcome any meeting just now. This was the first chance she'd had all day to be alone and get her thoughts together.

As far as losing Ernestina was concerned, Sarah personally didn't much care. The big Romney was not a painting she'd want to inherit. From what her aunt had said, Emma Kelling wasn't going to pine away for Ernestina and her dove, either. Family heirlooms abounded in the Kelling family, and they were more apt to be nuisances and bones of contention than unalloyed joys. Still, Ernestina belonged. It was the wanton, deliberate action of thievery that couldn't be tolerated. If only Max were here.

But he wasn't and he wouldn't be, not yet. She'd had a note from him this morning, scribbled at breakneck speed on hotel stationery from Lièges, saying he missed her like hell and had bought her a little souvenir. His last little souvenir had been a dainty gold filigree necklace set with chaste pearls and a few small diamonds, bought wholesale from a jeweler in Amsterdam who owed Max a favor. She'd love matching earrings, or some wonderful Finnish textiles for the new house they might some day build. Mainly, though, she wanted her husband.

She'd just have to want, though she hoped not for long. In the meantime she couldn't sit around watching a trail go cold even if she wasn't allowed to take the proper measures. She wished she could think of something more constructive than checking the windows, but she couldn't, so she went on.

Emma Kelling had two dining rooms in her house; more properly a formal large dining room and a breakfast room she preferred to use for small, informal meals whatever the hour. The latter was more convenient for the Heatherstones, being next to the butler's pantry. It was also far cozier, with its pale green walls and rosy chintzes. This was where Emma kept her luscious little Renoir and her wholesome Anders Zorn of a pink-cheeked girl eating a red-cheeked apple. This was where they'd eaten breakfast this morning and dinner last night. An ideal situation for drugging the Slepe-o-tite jug, Sarah thought. Only how could that have been managed without her knowing?

She shook her head and went on to the big dining room, a skating rink dominated by a vast black-walnut table and buffet, with matching chairs and side pieces enough to accommodate the whole Kelling clan, should it ever be possible to get them all sitting down in peace and amity. Sarah had had her own ups and downs with the relatives, but she'd always been on friendly terms with Aunt Emma's dining-room furniture, because of the lions.

The buffet had a shaggy lion's head in high relief roaring out of its towering back, and bas-reliefs of a whole pride decorating the cabinet doors. The table had great, flaring legs like a lion's haunches, ending in paws with the toes and talons meticulously defined. The ponderous apron was about a foot deep, ribbed and swirled and curlicued all over to suggest a lion's mane. Slipping in here alone to chat with the lions had been one of her childhood delights.

Tonight, though, Sarah found the lions standoffish and the deep wine-colored velvet hangings oppres-

sive. Emma never bothered to replace them with
lighter ones for the summer. Any large-scale entertaining she did during the hot weather was more apt
to be an alfresco affair with many small tables dotted
about the lawn and the sun parlor. The tables and
their matching chairs would be rented, but Sarah
knew the buffet held a stack of pink tablecloths laun-
dered and ready for the summer's first lawn party.
She gave the roaring lion a pat for auld lang syne
and went back across the hall to the library.

This had been Uncle Bed's favorite room. Sarah
could recall sitting on his knee and being allowed to
cut the tip off his cigar with an elegant silver snipper.
The cigar had smelled lovely when she sniffed its
smooth, warm brown wrapper, less so when Uncle
Bed put a match to the big end and puffed.

Emma must cherish her memories here, too. She
often sat in the library, alone or with old friends like
Charlie Daventer. This was where she kept the big
silver-framed photograph of Uncle Bed looking stiff-
upper-lippish as Kellings were wont to do when having their pictures taken by professional photogra-
phers. He'd have been thinking about how much the
sitting was going to cost, and wondering why a snap-
shot from somebody's old box Brownie wouldn't have
done as well.

There were other photographs: graduation portraits of her cousins Young Bed and Walter Alexander, and of their wives and their children, and a
very grand one of Emma herself in evening dress
and a great many pearls. It was a wonderful room.
Sarah felt as if it had been desecrated when she
looked up from Uncle Bed's desk and saw what was
pinned to the screen outside the window.

Chapter 6

Here it was, the note she'd been expecting but hadn't really believed would come. The words weren't cut out of newspapers, they were printed with a calligraphy pen, not very well but strictly by the book. The message was short and clear. "We want $5,000."

Sarah was flabbergasted. Five thousand dollars for Ernestina? It was an insult to Romney. Then again, five thousand could seem like a lot of money when you didn't have it. Sarah knew that as well as anybody. Maybe this was some misguided crew who simply needed five thousand dollars and didn't think it quite nice to ask for more. More likely, they had no idea what the painting was worth and assumed five thousand dollars was a sum Emma Kelling could be pried loose from without too much fuss. Or else this was just a prelude to a larger demand.

Whatever it was, it couldn't stay here. Sooner or later, some member of the cast would be dropping into the library for a respite from the hubbub and a nip from Uncle Bed's cellaret, which Aunt Emma kept filled with whiskey and gin for sentimental reasons. Sarah tried to raise the screen, but it was the old-fashioned wooden kind that had to be got at from outside the house. She let herself out one of the side doors and ran around to the library windows.

It was an exercise in futility. She might have remembered she wouldn't be able to reach that note from the ground; the house sat too high on its foundation. How had it been pinned there in the first place? She looked around the lawn for footprints, but there were none to be seen. The lawn was too well-kept to take them. Sarah did find a broken twig on one of the arborvitae that masked the foundation, but that didn't tell her anything except that the window must have been got at by somebody climbing up from the ground. Thus ruling out stilts and levitation, she supposed, for whatever that might be worth.

Back when there'd been a gardener, he'd kept his ladders in the potting shed, a red-brick octagon with a silly domed roof, set off by itself at the bottom of the garden. She supposed they must still be there, found on investigation that they were, and lugged the most portable of them back up to the house. She felt awfully conspicuous propping it against the window in this burglar-conscious neighborhood but at least she belonged to the household. What about the person who'd climbed up here to attach the note to the screen? It must have been done sometime today, in broad daylight. Otherwise Heatherstone would have found it when he drew the curtain this morning.

Sarah mounted the ladder, wondering what sort of story she could make sound halfway plausible if some member of the group inside happened to spot her. Getting the note off the screen was no problem, anyway. It had merely been hung there by means of two paper clips linked together, one attached to the small sheet of paper, one bent to form a hook with its free end poked through the mesh. Carefully, she noted. It hadn't made a hole.

She must remember to hold the note by the paper clips in case of fingerprints. If Max were here, he'd know how to test for them. Sarah supposed she could make a stab at it herself, but what would be the good? Even if she didn't ruin the evidence, she could hardly go around fingerprinting the cast for com-

parison without exciting remark, to say the ultimate
least. Especially not now, with everybody so edgy
over losing Charlie and having to break in a new
Notary practically on the eve of the performance.

Anyway, she had the note. Now to put away the
ladder and sneak back to the rehearsal without attracting attention. That turned out to be a bit of a
problem. There was a fairly stiff breeze now, and it
was flapping the paper up around her hand. By the
time she got the note back to the house, the only
fingerprints would be her own. It would probably
have made more sense to take the note in first and
then carry the ladder down to the potting shed, but
she hadn't thought of that in time and wasn't about
to turn back now. She'd see if she could find two
pieces of glass or something in the shed to lay the
paper between.

Sarah didn't mind an excuse to stay and poke
around. The potting shed had always been one of her
favorite places. She'd spent whole mornings and
afternoons here when she was little, watching the
gardener mixing his soils and cleaning his tools. Mr.
Hosbin had been getting on in years by then; she
supposed he'd been happy enough to putter around
entertaining a child instead of going outside and
doing the work he was getting paid for. Sarah had
never thought of him as a friend, though; their re-
lationship had been polite but formal. British by
birth, Mr. Hosbin had known his place and expected
his employer's niece to keep hers. That was all right.
Sarah's parents had treated her much the same way.

The potting shed had a general flavor of mild de-
cay about it nowadays. Sarah could see dust on the
counters and cobwebs around the ceiling. She supposed the place didn't get used much since the jolly
men from the landscaping service had taken over.
Aunt Emma had been in the habit years ago of going
out with a green rubber kneeling pad, a big straw

hat, and flowered gardening gloves with green thumbs to pull weeds from the rockery, but she probably didn't bother these days. What with her committees and her blood pressure, she wouldn't have much time for gardening. The jolly men would keep the area respectable with easily grown annuals and the rare plants would have gone to Emma's son Walter and his nice wife, Cynthia, who loved to garden.

It would be Young Bed who'd inherit this place, Sarah thought, and then who? Little Bed wouldn't want it, his ambition was to own a cattle ranch in Wyoming. An odd profession for a Kelling, but then Kellings were often odd. Sarah herself knew she was considered to be among the oddest now that she'd turned her Beacon Hill brownstone into a boardinghouse, turned the boardinghouse over to Cousin Brooks and his wife, and married out of the tribe. Brooks, to be sure, had picked a more unlikely spouse and so had Cousin Dolph but Theonia and Mary didn't count so much. Wives took their husbands' positions.

That was fine with Sarah. She loved her new husband's position. The relatives she cared about were accepting Max either for her sake or for his own, and the rest could go scratch themselves.

She'd forgotten what an intriguing place the potting shed was. Here was where Hosbin had been wont to whack Aunt Emma's rootbound plants out of their pots and put them into bigger ones, or else pick up a big knife and chop the root ball into sections to create a whole family of plants where one had been before. He'd explained at vast length why a good potting soil should contain both rich humus and sharp builder's sand. Sarah had never been able to figure out why he'd called sand sharp. To her, it was plain gritty.

She went rummaging through the drawers Hosbin had always kept so tidy, finding lots of staking twine and plant labels but no small squares of glass to protect the ransom note. Here was a notebook he'd recorded his bulb plantings in, she could slip the note between the pages. French hyacinths had been his main preoccupation in 1952, evidently. She was trying to read the neat handwriting by the dim light that filtered through the small, high, none too clean windows when the sack went over her head.

At first she thought it was just a blueberry net that had fallen off an overhead shelf. As she tried to push it away from her face, though, the cloth was yanked down over her arms, her hands grabbed from behind and tied together somewhat ineptly because she was putting up the best fight she could manage. She did land one good kick on her assailant's shins, but she had her old sneakers on so it couldn't have hurt much. All it accomplished, apparently, was to annoy her attacker. He, or a pretty strong she, grabbed Sarah by the shoulders, spun her around till she was dizzy, then suddenly let her go.

She didn't fall, but she staggered and gave her knee a crack on the drawer she'd left open. By the time she got her balance, she'd heard the door slam and realized she was alone.

Of all the hackneyed, melodramatic tricks to fall for! It must have been the writer of the note who trapped her, but why? An amateur, surely. Her wrists weren't even tied tight, she could wiggle them back and forth. Some of that old staking twine, she'd bet. That shouldn't be hard to break. She felt around till she encountered a tool of some kind—a hoe, she thought—and rubbed the strands against its sharpened edge until they parted. Then she pulled off the sack and tried the door. It didn't budge.

That didn't surprise her. She'd left the key lying on the counter, having retrieved it in the first place from its not very inspired hiding place on a nail around the corner. Sarah hoped her assailant had left it sticking in the lock outside instead of chucking it away in the compost heap or somewhere. Getting the locksmith out here to cut another would be a nuisance and an expense. She was Kelling enough to mind such things.

As to getting out of the shed, that was no great problem. Hadn't her jailer thought of the windows? They were inconveniently high, to be sure, and pretty narrow but then so was she. Sarah got the ladder she'd just brought back, set it against a window that she was almost sure didn't have raspberry canes planted underneath, and went to work.

The window was the kind that swings open from the bottom on hinges and gets propped up with a plant stick on hot days. This one clearly hadn't been opened since Hosbin retired and went home to die some fifteen years ago. Aunt Emma was still mailing his pension checks to a village in the Cotswolds and still getting back notes saying hers of recent date had arrived safely and hoping she was well with respectful compliments. Sarah blew about half a swarm of dead bees off the narrow ledge and climbed back down to find something to pry with.

It wasn't much of a struggle, actually, though she felt like a letter going through a mail slot. She did lose a few square inches of skin from her back when her jersey rode up as she squirmed her way over the sill. She'd been right about the raspberry canes, fortunately, but the ground was harder than she'd anticipated and she landed with a jolt that rattled her teeth. All things considered, though, her adventure had cost her little except a loss of temper and time.

Wrong. She'd also lost the ransom note. Was the key in the lock? Yes, it was. She opened the door and went back in, not without a qualm. No, the note was no longer on the counter where she'd put it down. It wasn't inside Mr. Hosbin's bulb book. It wasn't on the floor. It wasn't anywhere here. Her assailant must have taken it away. But why?

Because she was the wrong person to have found it? Because he'd found out how much Ernestina was worth and wanted to up the ransom? Because he'd remembered a trifle too late that paper can take fingerprints and that even calligraphy might be distinctive? Its very ineptness might be a clue. Suppose the one who did it was known to be starting a course, for instance, or had been seen buying the right sort of pen at a local stationer's. Or suppose he happened to be an art student.

Sarah wished she could be sure whether it had been one person who attacked her in the shed. It almost seemed as if there must have been two, one to drag that sack over her head and one to tie her hands. But it had been such a sloppy job. That business of spinning her around to make her dizzy so whoever it was could make a clean getaway hadn't been so sloppy, though, amateur or not. As for the careless tying-up, perhaps it hadn't been meant as anything more than another delaying tactic, to make doubly sure she didn't escape from the potting shed until her assailant or assailants could get back to the house and mingle with the rest of the cast.

It had been somebody from the house, Sarah was convinced of that. She must have been under surveillance while she was up on the ladder getting the note off the screen, maybe even earlier while she was prowling through the house. She didn't think she'd been followed, though. It was far more likely somebody had been keeping an eye on the note from the sun parlor. Like most houses of its period, Emma's had a good many nooks and jogs. From most angles the library windows couldn't be seen, but there was one at the far end that gave a clear view, and having the buffet table out there provided a perfect excuse to hang around, or at least pop back and forth. If two or more people were involved, maintaining a lookout would be no great trick at all.

She thought it would be safe to rule out the orchestra. Sir Arthur Sullivan's scoring wasn't complicated enough to allow for the musicians' mysterious backings and forthings that used to bewilder Sarah when she was twelve and using up the remains of her mother's last season's ticket at Symphony. They simply came in together, sat down together, played together until there was nothing left for them to play, and then went out together.

With the cast it was a different story entirely. Even a member of the chorus could be involved, Sarah assumed until she got back to the house and found Lady Sangazure and Sir Marmaduke just beginning their duet. That meant the entire chorus, both men and women, had been hard at work hailing the betrothal of Alexis the brave and the lovely Aline while she was skinning her wrists on that hoe and her back on the potting-shed windowsill. Aline and the girls would have come in first. Jenicot would have sung "Happy Young Heart," then the male chorus must have ushered in Alexis so that the lovers could fling themselves into each other's arms with whoops of rapture. Jenicot and Peter were still together, not embracing but standing quietly under the mock portrait waiting for their next cue.

"Welcome joy, adieu to sadness! As Aurora gilds the day, so those eyes, twin orbs of gladness chase the clouds of care away," Jack was informing Emma, who was taking it calmly. He wasn't flushed or panting, either, not like a man who'd just been tearing across the back lawn locking his fair lady's niece in the potting shed.

Both Sebastian Frostedd and Ridpath Wale, on the other hand, might have been doing whatever they chose. The rector had gone offstage some time ago, and the Sorcerer didn't even make his appearance until after the duet, the ensemble, and the solo in

which Alexis proclaims his love for the love that
loves for love alone.

Gillian Bruges hadn't had anything to do for quite
some time, either. She was leaning against the door
to the sun parlor, looking slightly annoyed, presumably because Jack was perforce giving his attention
to Emma instead of to her. Sarah went over and
spoke to her.

"Not getting along terribly fast, are we? What
happened?"

"Oh, weren't you here? They ran into problems
with the 'Happy Young Heart' number."

"You mean Aline's solo? Jenicot was all right yesterday."

Gillian shrugged. "Maybe your aunt was hoping
she could be a little better than all right today. I
thought Mrs. Kelling was being rather hard on Jenicot, myself. You can't expect a person to give more
than she's got, can you?"

Sarah didn't know what to say to that, so she only
smiled and went back to watching Aunt Emma and
Jack Tippleton. They were a pair of polished old sta-
gers, all right. Still, she could hear the little cracks
in Emma's voice, and the notes that didn't quite get
reached. This year she'd get by on personality and
savoir faire. Emma knew it, Jack knew it. Next year
the audience would have known it, and would have
given their applause out of kindhearted pity for the
old girl who didn't know when to quit. Sarah clapped
like anything when they'd finished the duet, and ran
over to hug her aunt in defiance of protocol.

Now came Frederick Kelling's big moment. He
cleared his throat, adjusted his pince-nez, and announced if not in tune at least in time with the music
that all was prepared for sealing and for signing. He
was going to be fine. Sarah still had her arm around
Aunt Emma, and could feel the older woman's muscles relax. From then on, there was no letdown.

Emma drove her cast, not precisely without mercy because she'd never have been capable of that, but with a brisk efficiency that would have suited the proprietor of a ladies' seminary she'd been mistaken for in *Iolanthe*.

By the time they started the second act, Mrs. Heatherstone had gone over to the carriage house. Sarah was kept busy brewing fresh pots of coffee and tea and refreshing the buffet, which continued to be visited by players whom nervousness had turned into constant nibblers, by those who'd been too keyed up to eat earlier and were hungry now, and by those who just wanted an excuse to hang around on the fringes and unload their personal critiques into a sympathetic ear. Her biggest job, actually, was providing the requisite ear. It wasn't always sympathetic, but she'd had plenty of experience soothing ruffled feathers at family gatherings and knew when not to tell the truth without having to lie.

All in all, it was an exhausting business and it went on a long, long time. Sarah was ready to faint with relief when at last they polished off the finale to Emma's modified satisfaction, found their wraps, and cleared out. All but Cousin Frederick.

Chapter 7

"Come on, Sarah," he yipped like a fussy old terrier, "you'll have to drive me home."

"So late?" Emma protested. "Can't you stay here, Fred? I'd be glad to give you a bed."

"Emma, I do not want your bed. I want my own bed. Get your coat, Sarah."

Arguing with an elderly relative who'd made up his mind to do as he chose regardless of what another elderly relative thought was best for him would be, as Sarah knew from bitter experience, a totally hopeless waste of time. She got her coat and found her car keys.

"Please don't wait up for me, Aunt Emma. I can let myself in."

"All right, dear. I have had rather a long day. Drive carefully."

Emma kissed her niece and went upstairs. Sarah and Frederick went out to the car. He didn't say anything till they'd got out to the main road, then he barked, "Turn left."

"But your house is to the right," Sarah objected.

"We're not going to my house. We're going to Charlie's."

"Charlie Daventer's? Whatever for?"

"Because in spite of all that yammering about micturitional syndrome Sebastian Frostedd was getting off back there, I know damned well Charlie did not get up last night to go to the bathroom, become dizzy upon voiding, and fall and whack his head on the bathtub, that's why."

"Cousin Frederick, how could you possibly?"

"Sarah, kindly remember that Charlie and I were closely acquainted for approximately sixty-eight years. I believe I can safely say I was as much in his confidence as any person now alive, your Aunt Emma not excluded. I know he'd been suffering badly from gout even before he became actually incapacitated. I know his kidneys were in the usual condition for a man his age, which is to say that he had to pass water too damned often for comfort. I also know how an old man feels when he has to leave his warm bed and stagger to the bathroom at least twice a night before his bladder pops. Add these factors together and what do you have?"

Without giving Sarah a chance to do so, Cousin Frederick delivered the answer. "You have an old man who has to pee and is reluctant to get up, do you not? You also have an old man, although perhaps you didn't know this, who has inherited a solid-silver *pot de chambre* with matching lid, said to have been sat on by no less a personage than General Lafayette on his return to the United States of America as guest of the nation in 1784. Charlie came to the conclusion some time ago that what was good enough for Lafayette was good enough for him. Not to put too fine a point on it, Sarah, I want to see what's in that pot."

"Oh, Frederick! What a revolting idea. Surely it would have been emptied now in any case."

"By whom?"

"Wasn't it the cleaning woman who found the body?"

"That is my understanding, but what makes you think she'd have done any cleaning today? She'd have been too busy calling the police and having palpitations. Furthermore, why should she work when

her employer was no longer alive to pay her? And
lastly, what makes you think she'd know the pot had
been used? You must realize, Sarah, that a man re-
sents having to give way to his infirmities and that
a chamber pot, regardless of its intrinsic value or
historical associations, is not the sort of article a
person of taste parks on the mantelpiece."

"I shouldn't have supposed so, but one never
knows. Where did Charlie keep his?"

"Next to his bed, in a dry sink that belonged to
his grandmother. It has a cupboard which was ex-
pressly designed for such a receptacle, contrary to
what modern decorators seem to think. Where else
could it be more conveniently got at when need arose?
Have I made my point?"

"Unfortunately, yes," Sarah had to answer. "Then
you think what I—"

She stopped, but too late. Frederick caught the
slip.

"Ah, then you agree with me that Charlie may
have been done away with. May I ask why, other
than the fact that you've been attracting foul play
of late faster than a dog picks up fleas?"

"There's that, I suppose. But the main reason is—
and for heaven's sake don't breathe a word of this to
a soul—Ernestina was stolen last night."

"Ernestina?" Frederick yelped. "You mean the big
Romney? How did it happen?"

"We don't really know. She was gone when Heatherstone went in this morning to draw the curtains.
A newspaper clipping about holding artworks for
ransom was thumbtacked inside the empty frame. I
found another ransom note hung on the library screen
this afternoon. Aunt Emma doesn't know about that
one yet."

Now that the cat was out of the bag, Sarah decided
she'd better give Cousin Frederick a complete run-
down. She told him about the Slepe-o-tite, and about

what had been happening to her in the potting shed while he was being introduced to Charlie Daventer's role.

"So you see," she finished, "it's simply too much of a coincidence that Charlie got killed last night."

"But why Charlie?"

"I can't imagine. However, he was at the house yesterday, and he did stay to dinner, along with Ridpath Wale. I forget how the talk got around to Ernestina, but anyway it did. About who she was, you know, and how valuable a Romney that size would be today. Then Charlie said Ernestina looked as if she could use a bath and Ridpath offered to give Aunt Emma the name of the person who'd cleaned his Sargents, but Aunt Emma said she didn't want to be bothered until after she'd got the show over with. I know it doesn't sound like much of a connection, but there it is."

"How much of this does Emma know?"

"Just the part that happened last night. I wanted to call the police, but she wouldn't let me on account of the publicity. She's made up her mind to keep quiet about the whole thing until after the show. That's why I got you to help me whip off that silly painting today, so people wouldn't see the empty frame and start asking questions. Frederick, did you know she'd decided this will be her last performance?"

"Balderdash. Emma will go on forever."

But Frederick didn't mean it, and Sarah knew he didn't. Neither of them said much after that until they reached the huge brick house, long ago remodeled into apartments, where Charles Daventer had lived and presumably died. The place was all in darkness, as might have been expected at such an hour. Sarah looked up at the black windows with no enthusiasm.

"How do you expect to get in, Frederick?"

"With a key, naturally. Charlie gave me one quite

some time ago. He liked company to help him pass the time while he was laid up, but it was agony for him to get up and open the door so he got me to have some duplicate keys made and hand them out to a few of his cronies. Emma has one, I know. She's been going over every day with his meals packed in a picnic basket. Emma's going to miss Charlie. So am I. Dammit, Sarah, it's hell to get old. Too bad the two of them didn't get married after Bed died."

"Oh, I doubt if that would have worked. What about yourself, Frederick? Isn't there some nice woman around you'd like to live with?"

"Me? I'm not the marrying kind. Anyway, who'd want a cantankerous old fogey?"

"You'd be surprised. Look at Dolph."

"That was one for the book, all right. I cannot for the life of me see why a fine woman like Mary ever tied herself up to that pompous oaf. I expect I'm jealous because she didn't pick me instead," Frederick added with a shamefaced little smile. "Well, come on. Let's get it over with."

Luckily, Charlie had lived in a first-floor apartment with a separate entrance. The other tenants weren't likely to hear them come in. Nevertheless, Sarah wasn't liking this a bit. Today had been brutal, tomorrow would be worse. Now she was expected to discover whether a chamber pot with an illustrious background had been put to its appropriate but unattractive use and thus turned a regrettable accident into a possible homicide. After that, she still had to deliver Frederick and get herself back to bed before the neighbors phoned the police or Aunt Emma called out the militia.

After a little fumbling Charlie got the door open. He switched on a light, and motioned Sarah inside. Here was another old bachelor's apartment, Sarah thought, though a far less austerely furnished one than her cousin's. The chief ornaments were photographs: a large one of Emma looking regal, older ones that must have been Charlie's parents and relatives, one of a young man in naval uniform. That would be his older brother, who'd gone down on a destroyer during World War II. Poor Charlie, he hadn't had much left except his friendships. And his money, Sarah supposed. There seemed to be no lack of comfort here. No doubt Aunt Emma had taken a hand in the decorating.

Charlie had owned a number of fine old pieces, some of them as early as his *pot de chambre*. Sarah couldn't stop to examine them because Frederick was hustling her into the bedroom. On their way they passed an open bathroom door that must have been where the cleaner found his body. Sarah noticed a fuzzy blue rug on the floor, rumpled into a heap. Nobody had bothered to straighten it after they took the body away. Probably the cleaner hadn't wanted to go in there.

Somebody had made Charlie's bed, though. When he saw that, Cousin Frederick uttered a word he must have learned from the boys at school. He knelt in front of the dry sink, opened the bottom cupboard, and drew forth the object of their search, lifted the heavy silver lid, and grunted with a sort of unhappy satisfaction.

"What did I tell you? Look here, Sarah."

"Must I?"

"Don't be squeamish. I want a witness."

Sighing, Sarah obliged. "I do see what you mean, Frederick," she had to admit. "Poor Charlie must have spent a restless night. Unless he'd forgotten to empty it yesterday morning."

"Don't be ridiculous. Charlie was no damned yahoo. If he couldn't manage the job himself, he'd have got the visiting nurse to clean it. She's been coming in every morning since his foot began giving him hell. Kept tabs on the medication, helped him shave,

got him into the shower. That's another thing, you
know. Did you happen to notice that bathroom off
the front hall?"

"Yes. I assume that's where the woman found him."

"It is, but it's not the bathroom Charlie was in the
habit of using. There's another in the back hall. It
used to be just a flush and a sink, but when Charlie
got so he couldn't climb in and out of the bathtub
without banging his sore toe, he had a stall shower
installed out there. He liked it better, anyway.
Claimed it was handier."

"But the other one is nearer."

"No it isn't. See?"

Frederick opened a door that Sarah had supposed
must be a closet. Sure enough, it led to a fairly spacious back entry from which the kitchen and another
room led off. Directly beside the bedroom door was
the small bathroom no doubt intended for the use of
the live-in maid who'd surely have been part of the
original household.

"That does it," said Sarah. "We've got to call the
police."

Chapter 8

"At this hour?" Frederick protested.

"If we wait till morning, somebody's likely to come in here and tidy up. If that pot gets emptied, you'll have no case whatever. Who other than Charlie and yourself and perhaps the visiting nurse would have known he used it during the night?"

"That's hard to say. I doubt very much he'd have told Emma. In fact, I don't suppose Charlie would have told anybody at all if he didn't have to. The only reason I found out is that I happened to be here one day when his foot was really giving him Hail Columbia. He heard the call of nature. I offered to help him to the bathroom, but he was just too miserable to make the attempt, so he asked me to hand him the pot. Charlie tried to make a joke of the performance, you know, but I could tell he was embarrassed. One doesn't much like admitting one's unable to cope with one's bodily functions in the usual way."

"Naturally not. Shall I call the police, or will you?"

"Young woman, with a bit more practice, you could turn into a worse nag than Cousin Mabel. I suppose I'd better do it. They know me down at the station. On a purely social basis, I hasten to add."

There was a telephone beside Charlie's bed, but for some reason Frederick didn't want to use it. He left Sarah there to guard the evidence and went to

83

the extension in the room out back that Charlie had no doubt called his den.

A car was there in less than five minutes. The Pleasaunce police must be as efficient as Aunt Emma claimed they were. They were intelligent, too; at least the one who showed up was. His name was Detective Sergeant Formsby, and he didn't take a minute to grasp the significance of Cousin Frederick's unlovely clue.

"I expect Mr. Daventer'd been having urinalysis tests for his gout. I'll have this tested to make sure it checks out, and see what the visiting nurse says about when the pot was last emptied. But you know something, Mr. Kelling? I think we're going to find you're one hundred percent right and it doesn't surprise me a bit. Frankly, some of us weren't too happy with the accident finding. That was a mighty well-defined dent Mr. Daventer got in his skull, and there are no hard edges in that bathroom. Come on, I'll show you what I mean."

The three of them trooped across to where the body had been found. Formsby snapped on the overhead light. The bathroom was small and the arrangement simple. An old-fashioned iron tub with high sides and a rounded-over edge was set to the left of the door. A more modern porcelain basin, molded all in curves to look functional, stood beside it at the back, and the flush closet was tucked discreetly away at the far side. There wasn't even a stool to trip over, and the wastebasket was a flimsy thing of blue plastic.

"We found the body right about here."

Formsby obliged by flopping down on the crumpled blue rug with his head in the corner between the sink and the tub.

"Now you'll notice what I said about no hard edges on the fixtures. The woman who found him testifies that he was lying on his back the way I did just now, with the rug wrinkled up under his feet. It looked as if he'd slipped on the rug and fallen as he turned to leave the room, presumably after having washed his hands, and whacked his head either on the sink or on the edge of the tub. The rug does have a rubber nonskid backing, but it's a fairly flimsy affair, like all those washable rugs, and it will bunch up if you happen to kick it the wrong way. Tripped would be a better word than slipped, I guess, assuming he did either."

"There was no mark of any kind on the fixtures?" Sarah asked him. "No trace of blood or hair?"

"Not a thing. The wound didn't break the skin, though, and he didn't have a heck of a lot of hair anyway, so that didn't exactly count as a suspicious circumstance. As you most likely know, falls in the bathroom are a common cause of household fatalities. Mr. Daventer being alone in the apartment with his pajamas on, not what you'd call a young man and maybe none too steady on his feet from the gout, it was reasonable enough to consider the death accidental from the lack of any real evidence to the contrary. If we'd known about this—er—receptacle—"

"But you didn't," said Frederick. "Nobody can fault you for that. I doubt whether the cleaning woman even knew. If she did, I suppose she thought it wasn't a nice thing to talk about. In any event, she must have known he'd been on the mend, so she'd have found it natural enough for him to get up and go to the bathroom. She might conceivably have wondered why he chose this one instead of the other, which he was more in the habit of using. Then again, she mightn't. She's not a housekeeper, you know, just somebody who came in by the hour to sling a mop around."

"So she said," Formsby agreed. "She didn't seem

to know much about Mr. Daventer as a person, just that he got mean if she didn't dust to suit him."

"There you are," said Frederick. "Does that sound like a man who'd leave a pisspot unemptied?"

"Please, Frederick," said Sarah. "You've made your point."

Formsby smiled. "Miss Kelling, would you mind telling me how you happen to be in on this? Were you a friend of Mr. Daventer's, too?"

"I'm Mrs. Bittersohn, actually," Sarah corrected. "Mrs. Max Bittersohn. No, I wasn't a friend of Mr. Daventer, but I did see him yesterday. I'm staying with my aunt, Mrs. Beddoes Kelling. She's putting on one of her Gilbert & Sullivan operettas, and Mr. Daventer was to have taken part. He was at the house yesterday to rehearse, and stayed to dinner. He didn't have too much to drink, I can testify to that. Not that he would anyway, I don't suppose, but my aunt was keeping a sharp eye on him because of his gout, you know. She wanted him in good shape for the performance. I'm sure she also chased him home in time to get a good night's rest, though I can't say precisely when. I left about half-past eight, myself. To visit Cousin Frederick, as a matter of fact. Mr. Daventer was certainly gone by the time I got back, which was about eleven o'clock."

"How did Mr. Daventer get back and forth? Did he drive himself?"

"I couldn't say. I was out in the sun parlor painting scenery when he arrived. Some other people got to my aunt's house at more or less the same time, so I suppose he may have got a ride with one of them. Ridpath Wale, who's playing the Sorcerer, stayed to dinner also. If Charlie didn't have a car, I expect Ridpath brought him home."

"He wouldn't have taken a taxi?"

"Never in a million years. If there'd been no other ride available, my aunt would have either brought him herself or sent him in her car with her chauffeur. I can find out in the morning, if you want."

"I'd appreciate it. This Mr. Wale you mentioned, were he and Mr. Daventer on friendly terms?"

"That was my impression. I don't know how much you know about the Pirates of Pleasaunce, but they're mostly old friends of my aunt, or their children or nephews or whatever. Frederick, you can help Sergeant Formsby on this better than I. What he's really asking is whether Charlie had any mortal enemies."

"Other than Cousin Mabel, you mean?"

This was an exceedingly ill-timed jest. Sergeant Formsby pounced on it. "Who's Cousin Mabel? That wouldn't be Miss Mabel Kelling of 47 East Pleasaunce Drive?"

"Yes," Sarah admitted. "Do you know her?"

Stupid question. Cousin Mabel called the police at least three times a week on the average, to complain about one thing or another.

"But she wasn't Mr. Daventer's enemy, Sergeant. Not more than anybody else's, at any rate. My cousin was only joking. Weren't you, Frederick?"

"That is correct, Sergeant Formsby. I was joking, in the same sense as one might joke about bubonic plague or the Johnstown Flood. If in fact Mabel Kelling ever did decide to murder someone, she'd be more apt to pick on me than on Charlie Daventer. Miss Kelling, who, I'm relieved to say, is not my first cousin but merely a third cousin once removed, which is less of a removal than I could wish, had a certain tendresse for Charlie."

"A tendresse, eh?"

"The sort of tendresse a hungry tigress might entertain for a particularly toothsome gazelle," Frederick amended. "That is an ungentlemanly statement, Sergeant. I propose to amplify it into outright caddishness. Mabel Kelling has the collector's instinct. The one thing she has so far never succeeded in collecting is a husband. She looked upon Charlie as a collectible."

"I see. Was there ever what you'd call a—"

Sergeant Formsby was clearly nonplussed as to what one might call it. Sarah, worn out as she was and worried as she well might have been, had to laugh.

"Sergeant Formsby, you're not thinking about a *crime passionnel?* Can you picture Charles Daventer entertaining Mabel Kelling in his pajamas in the middle of the night? Let me assure you, it would never happen. Our cousin has never given anything away in her life. There's no chance whatever she'd sell her virtue, assuming anyone wanted it, for less than full price. And Charlie wouldn't have been willing to pay, because he was in love with my Aunt Emma."

The detective smiled at that. "Name me somebody around here who isn't. Your aunt and Mr. Daventer weren't planning to get married or anything, were they?"

"Oh no, nothing like that. It was just one of those worshiping-from-afar things that had been going on for years and years. My aunt was fond of Charlie as a friend, but she never really cared for any man except my Uncle Beddoes. As for Charlie, I think hopeless adoration suited him just fine, if you want the truth."

"Yeah, I can see where it might have its advantages. Then Mrs. Kelling must feel pretty bad about losing Mr. Daventer."

"Oh yes, but she's not one to give way to her feelings. The show will go on as scheduled, if that's what you're wondering."

"Well, I was, kind of. My wife and I've had our tickets for quite a while. We always look forward to it. Have you got somebody to take Mr. Daventer's part?"

"Me, unfortunately," Frederick told him. "He was playing an old curmudgeon and I happened to be the only curmudgeon available at the moment, so Emma nabbed me."

"How did you happen to be available at the moment? Does that mean you were present in the house?"

Sarah and Frederick refrained from catching each other's eye. They had no definite reason as yet to link Charlie's death with the theft of Ernestina. Emma Kelling had specifically insisted she didn't want the police told the Romney was gone until after the show. It was her show and her Romney. Frederick told the truth, but not the whole truth.

"Sarah's been painting the scenery. She'd called me over there to help her with a last-minute project. As it happened, she and I'd been working at the back of the house and were the last of the group to hear about Charlie's death, though I don't suppose that's at all relevant. Anyway, I daresay Emma could have dragooned some fellow from the chorus to do the role, but that would have left them a man short, so she put the arm on me. Mine's a smaller part than theirs, actually."

"I see. Have you appeared in any of the Pirates' previous performances?"

"No, and I don't expect to be asked again."

"What about Mr. Daventer? Was he one of the regulars?"

"I expect likely. He'd have walked across hell on a rotten rail if Emma asked him to."

"He'd appeared occasionally in minor roles," Sarah amplified.

"Was he well-liked among the cast? You don't know if there's been any ill feeling because he got the part somebody else wanted, or anything like that?"

"Sergeant Formsby, this isn't grand opera. If they'd run into somebody else who wanted to look old and ugly and mumble a line or two here and there, I'm sure both Charlie and my aunt would have been quite willing to let him. As to fighting, there simply hadn't been time, assuming my aunt would have stood for it. Charlie'd been laid up with gout, you know, ever since the first couple of rehearsals and everybody was relieved that he was well enough to show up yesterday. Rather than wanting to do him in, I should say every member of the cast was praying he'd be able to hang together until after the performance."

"But you can't say for sure."

"No, I can't," Sarah had to admit. "I've only been out here since Monday and I've been busy with the scenery, so I haven't had much time to socialize with the players. I'd met some of them casually over the years, and others, especially the younger ones, not at all. I'm only giving you my impression for what it's worth."

"Well, I've known Charlie Daventer all my life, more or less," Frederick insisted, "and I'm fairly sure I'd know if he had a running feud on with anybody. Charlie and I didn't exactly sit in each other's pocket, but we've seen a fair amount of each other off and on, especially since he'd been laid up. I'd walk over to bring him his paper, pick up his mail, or just sit and yarn with him as old gaffers are far too prone to do."

"How did you get into the apartment tonight, Mr. Kelling?"

"Charlie'd given me a door key so I could come and go without his having to get out of bed and answer the door."

"That so? You don't know if he gave keys to any of his other friends?"

"Emma Kelling has one. So does Jack Tippleton, and I believe Ridpath Wale."

"What about Sebastian Frostedd?" Sarah prompted.

Frederick Kelling drew himself up to his full five feet six inches and gave her a schoolmasterish look. "I am quite sure Sebastian Frostedd does not have a key."

"These men you mentioned, they're all members of the cast?" Formsby asked.

"They are. They are also personal friends of long standing. To the best of my knowledge, they and Emma are the only people other than myself who were recently given keys. The cleaning woman may have had one. You'd know that better than I, since you've already talked to her. The only other possibility I can think of is the visiting nurse from whom he'd been getting daily attention. I don't know her name, I never met her. I tried to time my own visits so that Charlie would be alone when I came. He may even have had a different person every day. I don't know how these things work."

"I can check it out with the Visiting Nurses' Association."

Sergeant Formsby wrote himself a note. He had a blue-covered memo book with a spiral binding, Sarah noticed. Just like Aunt Emma's. She wondered if he kept the used ones in his wife's cedar chest.

He was hesitating, his pencil still touching the blue-lined paper. "Miss Mabel Kelling doesn't have a key, then?"

"Good God, no! Not unless she bullied it out of somebody else," Frederick amended, "which she's quite capable of doing. Come on, Sarah. Let's go find out."

"Cousin Frederick, we are not going to call on Cousin Mabel at this hour of the night. I'm dead on my feet, I still have to get you home, and get back myself before Aunt Emma wakes up and has a fit, if she hasn't had one already. Good night, Sergeant

Formsby. If you need us again, you know where to find us."

"Thanks, Mrs. Bittersohn. Oh hey, your husband doesn't happen to be the Max Bittersohn who cracked the Wilkins case?"

"Yes, he is. Do you know him?"

Formsby warmed up, as people were apt to do when they found out she was connected with Max. "We've met. He doesn't happen to be with you in Pleasaunce, by any chance?"

"I wish he were. He might be back soon. In the meantime, though, I'm afraid you'll have to make do with my cousin and me."

"Well, you two are doing okay so far. Ever work with your husband on a case, Mrs. Bittersohn?"

"How do you think I met him in the first place? As a matter of fact, we work together quite a lot. I'm pretty good at the bits and pieces. And may I point out that in this instance, Frederick and I are more likely to make headway on gathering information than you are. We can be nosing around among Mr. Daventer's personal acquaintances while you take care of the visiting nurse, the house-cleaner, and the neighbors. I'll be greatly surprised if this turns out to have been an outside job."

"What makes you say that?"

"It's most apt to be our nearer and dearer who do us in, isn't it? By the way, did you find Mr. Daventer's own door key?"

"The cleaner found it on the dresser with his other personal effects. With so many copies floating around, though, I don't suppose it would be hard for somebody to get hold of one long enough to have it duplicated."

"Assuming it was necessary," said Sarah. "Nobody'd take the risk, I shouldn't think, unless he had some pressing reason to get at Charlie. Or unless he was absolutely bats, of course. Even then he'd have had to be connected with Charlie in one way or another, shouldn't you think? One doesn't go around pinching keys on the off chance he'll find a door they fit, does one?"

"Who knows? Okay, Mrs. Bittersohn. See what you and Mr. Kelling can come up with, and we'll take it from there."

"We expect a favor in return, Sergeant Formsby."

"What's that?"

"No leaks to the press until after the show. As it is now, Frederick and I can grill the cast for all they're worth. If it gets around that you're investigating Charlie Daventer's death as a possible murder, they'll realize they're all potential suspects and haul in their horns, and we shan't get a yip out of anybody."

"Wouldn't you think they'd be willing to cooperate with the police like law-abiding citizens?"

Frederick Kelling emitted one of his more formidable snorts. "If you believe that, Sergeant Formsby, you're far too naive to be a detective. To begin with, as Sarah mentioned earlier, most of that crowd have known each other since Hector was a pup. Half of them are related in one way or another, and they'd all close ranks on general principles."

"Is that your only reason, Mr. Kelling? It wouldn't be the unfavorable publicity you're worried about, by any chance?"

"That's part of it, certainly," Sarah took it upon herself to answer. "All right, Sergeant, we'll come clean."

"Sarah," Frederick protested. "You told me yourself Emma doesn't want anybody to know."

"One doesn't hold out on the police, Frederick," Sarah replied primly, even though she was about to. "The thing of it is, Sergeant Formsby, this is going to be Emma Kelling's last performance. She realizes her age has finally caught up with her, and she wants to go out in a blaze of glory before her audience catches on. That's in strictest confidence and if you breathe one word to a soul, I'll go straight back to Boston and let you stew in your own juice. And I'll take Cousin Frederick with me."

Sergeant Formsby smiled. "Okay, Mrs. Bittersohn. Your aunt's done enough for this town, I guess she's entitled to a little consideration. You understand I can't hold up the investigation, though."

"We're not asking you to. We've already said we'll do everything we can to help. We'll even tackle Cousin Mabel for you," Sarah added recklessly.

"Now wait a minute," Frederick gulped.

"I will not wait. You were all for it a moment ago. Frederick, you needn't think you're going to weasel out on me now that you've got me into this. Anyway, I've been here all week and haven't so much as called her up yet, so I suppose I might as well try to get some good out of a visit if there's any to be got. You'll have to come with me and help me interrupt. You know one person alone can't possibly stem the flow once she gets wound up."

"Confound it, why did I have to remember that chamber pot? All right, Sarah, but on your own head be it."

Muttering angrily, Frederick followed Sarah out to her car. She delivered him to his meager dwelling, sat outside with the car lights on till she'd seen him safely inside, then drove herself back to Aunt Emma's.

She was ready with a glib, "Sorry to be so late. I stayed at Frederick's and we got to talking," but she didn't have to say it. With or without the inducement of Slepe-o-tite, everybody seemed to be asleep.

A hot shower would have been welcome after so long and messy a day, but Sarah didn't want to risk waking her aunt by running the water. She washed as quietly as she could, hauled her weary bones into bed, and started counting sheep. Worn out as she was, she had to prod upward of two thousand reluctant ovines over the pasture fence before her nerves quit jangling and let her drop off to sleep.

Chapter 9

Given her choice, Sarah would have stayed in bed half the morning, but that happy fate was not for her. Soaring above her tribulations, Emma Kelling was projecting her still-powerful contralto like a call to arms as she sailed out of her bedroom.

"Wild with adoration! Mad with fascination! To indulge my lamentation no occasion do I miss. Good morning, Heatherstone. Isn't that lazy niece of mine up yet? We'll soon fix that."

In self-defense Sarah shouted back, "I'm up." She might as well be. Otherwise, Aunt Emma would be serenading her with Uncle Bed's tuba.

At least she got her shower, or rather a hot wallow in the tub, taking a long time at it to soak out the leftover fatigue, giving herself a shampoo as part of the bargain. When she couldn't decently stall any longer, she used her aunt's hand dryer on her light brown hair, put on a denim skirt and a blue jersey, and went down.

"I thought I'd better do my hair while I had the chance." She kissed her aunt, who was already putting quince jam on a hot biscuit, and took her place. "Scrambled eggs and biscuits, please, Heatherstone. What's on the agenda for today, Aunt Emma?"

"First, we must get all those baskets and the costumes over to the auditorium. That's going to take us a few trips, I expect. Oh, and the makeup. You'll be running that department."

"Me? Aunt Emma, I can't possibly. I don't know the first thing about stage makeup."

"Nonsense. If you can paint scenery, you can surely paint a face. Think how much less area you'll have to cover. Anyway, some of us will want to do our own, I expect. I always do, myself. You'll get mostly the chorus, and you don't have to be quite so fussy with them. They're always hopping around with their mouths open, so the audience never gets a good look at them anyway."

Sarah gave up and ate her grapefruit. There was no earthly sense in arguing back once Aunt Emma had delivered a ukase. Oh well, she'd never painted scenery before, either, and that hadn't gone so badly.

"How do you propose to cart all that stuff, Aunt Emma?" she asked with a thought to her and Max's own lush upholstery. "You don't want to mess up the Buick."

"Heaven forfend! Heatherstone would resign on the spot. More coffee?" Without waiting for an answer, Emma Kelling refilled Sarah's cup from the wantonly begarlanded Bavarian pot she liked to see on her breakfast table. "Guy Mannering's supposed to be borrowing a station wagon. He has access to a wide variety of vehicles, it appears."

"I hope he doesn't steal them to fit the occasion," Sarah remarked, grinding fresh pepper over her scrambled eggs. "When's he due to arrive?"

"Any minute now, I should think."

Emma chatted on about their, or more specifically her, program for the day while Sarah went on with her breakfast. The costumes were being verbally pressed when the doorbell rang.

"That will be Guy now," said Emma. "Ask him if he'd care to join us for coffee, Heatherstone."

But it was not Guy. The man came back with a long, white florist's box.

"For you, Mrs. Kelling."

"What fun. I adore getting flowers. Oh, Sarah, I wonder if these could be from Charlie? He always used to, you know. He might have ordered them before he—"

Emma's voice broke a little, and she became extremely busy opening the box. It turned out to be full of gaudy orange and yellow gladioli. She looked relieved.

"Not from Charlie, surely. He always sent roses. Pink ones, you know. Red wouldn't have been proper, to a married woman. Now who can it be?"

She took the card out of its little envelope, glanced at the words written on it, and let it drop back among the flowers. "Heatherstone, take these things and toss them on the compost heap."

"Aunt Emma, what's the matter?" Sarah cried. "You're white as a ghost."

Mrs. Kelling picked up the note again and handed it over to Sarah. There again was the inexpert calligraphy. All it read was, "Have you got the money ready?"

"What money are they talking about?" she demanded.

Sarah had to tell. "Five thousand dollars. I found another note pinned to the screen on the library window yesterday afternoon. You were in the midst of rehearsing and I didn't want to upset you."

Her aunt's lips tightened. "Sarah Kelling, if there is one thing on this earth I positively cannot stand, it's having my feelings spared. Where is that note now?"

"They stole it back."

Sarah had to explain her sorry little adventure in the potting shed. Emma was, as she might have expected, only mildly aghast.

"Well, you seem to have managed better than I should have. I'd never in the world have been able to squeeze myself through those stupid little windows, and one must feel unbearably ridiculous hanging halfway out, screaming like a banshee. On second thought, Heatherstone, there's no sense in letting those perfectly good gladioli go to waste. Pop them in water till we're ready to leave. We can use them for the baskets in the foyer, the ones people will be dropping their candy wrappers and cigarette butts into."

She touched her napkin to her lips and laid it beside her empty plate. "I do hope we haven't made the mistake of cutting those daffodils a day too early so they'll be starting to wilt tomorrow. The problem is, we have the senior citizens and the children from Fred's school coming to the dress rehearsal and I don't see why they shouldn't have the good of them as much as anybody else. Heatherstone, don't forget to put in one of those big tin pitchers. We'll want it to soak the Oasis after we finish the baskets. If you're quite sure you don't want another biscuit, Sarah, you may as well start carrying down those spectres' shrouds from your bedroom."

By the time Sarah was back downstairs with her first ghostly armload, Guy Mannering had arrived with a station wagon belonging, he said, to his father, the English horn. Sarah took careful note of his expression as she handed him the pail of gladioli to be put in the back with the baskets. He didn't look anything but pleased to be of service. If she ever found the time, she'd have to get him aside and pump him about what he'd been doing last night, and with whom. Right now, according to Emma's blue notebook, she must load her own car with as many costumes as she could pack in without squashing and follow Guy over to the auditorium. Then she was to come back and get some more.

And forth she went and back she came, feeling like Noah's dove, and forth and back and forth again, sometimes passing Guy and exchanging honks en route. This was not the ideal way to conduct an interrogation. As the morning wore on, Sarah pretty much forgot what she'd been going to ask him, anyway. By the time she'd got her last and final load to the auditorium, an astonishing number of helpers had manifested themselves. Sarah couldn't tell whether so many hands were making light work or merely creating a state of worse confusion, but Aunt Emma was looking pleased in a frazzled sort of way, so she supposed it must be all right.

And things were visibly getting done. The programs were delivered and unpacked, the costumes shaken out and hung up in the dressing rooms. Lady Sangazure's bustle was parked in a safe corner where nobody could trip over it and squash it, a lopsided *derrière* being no part of Emma Kelling's game plan.

The makeup table was set up backstage with its pots and tubes and jars and brushes and sticks of greasepaint and a whole snowstorm of cotton balls, plus a wastebasket to chuck them into when they'd served their manifold purposes. Sarah herself thought of the wastebasket, and received loud accolades for her sagacity as an organizer. She forgot her stage fright over the makeup and found herself handling the sticks of greasepaint with cocky anticipation. She'd finished Sir Marmaduke's mansion; surely she'd have no trouble with Cousin Frederick's face, especially since she didn't have to do anything except make him look more like what he already was.

Oh dear, why did she have to think of Cousin Frederick? Now she remembered she'd intended to get Guy Mannering off by himself and grill him. No chance of that now. Guy was up to his ears and a good way beyond in scenery, and Aunt Emma was at her elbow, reminding her it was high time they started putting the flowers into the baskets.

So it was. Somehow or other, lunchtime had passed

and the afternoon was half shot. After a flurry of strained politeness over whether they should fix all the baskets together then lug them to their assigned places, or lug first and fix later, Sarah and a few others set to work amicably enough, hauling wet stems out of clammy buckets and poking them in among the prickly foliage she'd got so sick and tired of yesterday.

The varicolored flowers, even the extortionists' gladioli, did make a tremendous difference. By the time they were down to empty buckets and scraps of leftover vegetable matter, the house was looking as festive as the stage. All was prepared for sealing and for signing, for the rollicking bun and the gay Sally Lunn, and for the Sorcerer's too-potent potion.

Chapter 10

"Thank you, everyone. That's it for now." Emma Kelling picked up her handbag and began switching off lights. "Come along, Sarah. We've just time enough for a quick bite and a short nap. Seven o'clock sharp, everybody."

Sarah moved to join her aunt, but Guy Mannering was beside her. "Sarah, the crew and I are going out for hamburgers. We were sort of hoping you might like to join us."

All things considered, Sarah would have been happy to settle for a quiet hour in her now shroudless bedroom. Max never would, though; he'd grab at the chance to put in a spot of work on Guy Mannering. She made a quick switch from a sigh to a smile.

"Would you mind, Aunt Emma? I can run you back home first."

"No, go along with the boys and have some fun. I'll beg a lift with Jack and Martha." Emma brushed Sarah's cheek with her own, which felt like a baby's pillow, and went off in the familiar whiff of Parma Violet.

Sarah turned to Guy. "I'll be right with you. Give me two seconds to wash my hands."

Sarah didn't offer to drive, partly because she didn't want to deflate Guy's ego and partly because she didn't much care for the idea of all those painty jeans on her upholstery. She almost reconsidered, though, when she found the English horn's station wagon had somehow or other got traded back for the piccolo's truck.

Actually they managed well enough. Skip, the smallest and skinniest, climbed up on the ledge behind the seat and curled himself up like a caterpillar in a cocoon. Sarah squashed in under the gearshift between Guy and Chill, who had the build of a football tackle but informed her his real game was chess.

Back when she was sixteen or so, she'd probably have found this the greatest fun in the world, Sarah thought as they jounced over the well-kept road. What must it be like on a rough surface?

"How is it that your piccolo player friend owns a truck?" she asked, trying not to bite off her tongue in the process.

"It's his brother's, really," Guy explained. "He has a lawn service. You know, mowing lawns and that kind of stuff. Only in the summer."

"When else would you mow a lawn?" Skip jeered from his perch.

"You needn't get smart just because you go to Amherst," Chill told him.

It was banter of the lowest grade, but Sarah found it amusing enough. She egged them on with a question or a comment when they showed signs of running down, and tried to think of a way to steer the conversation around to hijacking paintings without scaring them off if they were guilty or giving anything away if they weren't.

The ride was longer than Sarah cared for. Eventually, though, they unpacked themselves at one of those eateries preferred by the young and the blunt of palate, and went in. Its *specialité de la maison* appeared to be double megaburgers and ultrathick shakes. Sarah pleaded feebly for a mere cheeseburger and a cup of black coffee.

The noise was just short of unendurable, the cuisine could most charitably be described as edible.

For all that, the place was rather fun. Among his peers, Guy forgot to be the blasé aesthete who'd nibbled fastidiously at Emma Kelling's watercress sandwiches while he discussed Vasari and Vivaldi without being quite clear as to which was who. He revealed a silly sense of humor and a gargantuan capacity for junk food. Sarah watched in stunned incredulity as he polished off his megaburger with french fries, a side order of onion rings, two thick shakes, and then ordered something called a Whooperdooper.

This proved to be three large scoops of varicolored ice creams with butterscotch, strawberry, and chocolate syrups, topped off with whipped cream, cherries, and a crumbled-up peanut candy bar. Skip had a Whizzerdizzer, at which Sarah tried not to look too closely, and Chill a Bananawanna. Sarah was toying with her own modest portion of peppermint ice cream, which she hadn't much wanted but felt she must order in the face of all this rampant gourmandizing, when another young man wearing a sweatshirt and a Peter Pan hat with a turkey feather in it stopped at their table.

"Hi, guys."

"Hi, Ed," the three male members of the party replied through respective mouthfuls of Whooperdooper, Whizzerdizzer, and Bananawanna. Guy struggled for a moment with his butterscotch, then managed to articulate, "Sarah, that's Eddie."

"Hi, Eddie." Sarah hoped this was the accepted etiquette.

Apparently it was. Eddie replied, "Hi, Sarah," hauled a chair up to the end of their table, sat on it backward without taking his hat off, and reached over to scoop up a bite of Chill's Bananawanna without being invited. "So what's new? Hey, how did you guys make out last night?"

"About what?" Skip replied.

"Hey, come on. You know what."

"Oh, that. Look, we can talk about it later, huh?"

"Huh? Oh, sure."

Eddie took another scoop of the Bananawanna, stood up, and spun the chair back to where he'd got it from. "Hey, I'll see you around. Nice to meet you, Sarah," and was gone before she could do more than smile and wave her spoon at him.

"I hope I didn't scare your friend away," she told Guy. "If there was something you people wanted to talk about, I could have made myself scarce for a few minutes."

"No, no, it wasn't anything, honestly. Just a— well, kind of a joke we were playing on somebody. Kid stuff, I'm afraid."

Guy was trying to recapture his *mondaine* image, and making a poor fist of it. He also appeared, at last, to have lost his appetite. He pushed the melting remnants of his Whooperdooper away as if he couldn't stand the sight of it any longer, and began waving at the waitress to bring their check.

"Come on, you two. We can't spend the night here."

"Why not?" demanded Chill, chasing the end of a banana through a sea of marshmallow sauce. "We're finished with the scenery, aren't we?"

"Yes you are," Sarah took it upon herself to reply. "You've done a marvelous job and I know my aunt will want to thank you personally. It's just that I have to get back to do the makeups. I've never tried it before, I don't know the first thing about it, and I've got to get all those different kinds of goop sorted out before I paint everybody the wrong color."

That set off the wisecracks again, as Sarah had hoped it would. She didn't care for the role of skeleton at the feast. Guy had been looking awfully glum there for a moment. Glum and something else. Could he be scared? What sort of joke had these jolly japesters been up to, and on whom had they been playing it?

After they'd got themselves packed into the truck, she asked them in what she hoped was a casual tone, "What time did you get to the auditorium this morning? Mrs. Heatherstone says you left my aunt's house practically at the crack of dawn."

"That's right," said Skip. "I might add we didn't see you there."

"No, I'm afraid I was still asleep. It wasn't really only seven o'clock, was it?"

"Well, maybe not exactly," Guy admitted. "Ten past, something like that. We spent maybe twenty minutes loading the flats, and got to the auditorium just as the janitor was opening up."

"So early?"

"Seven forty-five on the dot. He always does. He told us so."

"If you ever met his wife, you'd know why," said Chill. "Sheesh!"

"How do you know her?" Skip asked him.

"They go to our church. At least she goes, and drags him along with her."

"Like your mother drags you."

After that, there was no getting any sense out of them. Sarah didn't try, but concentrated on timing the run back in the hope of finding out how fast the truck could travel. Not very, was the best she could come up with. Assuming these three nice boys had managed to smuggle Ernestina out with the scenery, even though Mrs. Heatherstone swore they couldn't have, it hardly seemed possible they'd have had time to ditch her somewhere safe and still meet the janitor at a quarter to eight. Surely they wouldn't be stupid enough to lie about a fact so easily checked.

But if Ernestina was in fact the joke they'd pulled last night, why would they have left her in the house until morning? Because they couldn't get hold of the truck till then? That hardly seemed likely. To get such an early start, one would assume they must have borrowed it the night before.

Maybe they were pulling some crazy Tom Sawyer stunt, making it more difficult to enhance the artistic effect. Who knew? She tried another question, when she could make herself heard.

"Are you all art students?"

"Perish the thought," Skip told her. "Our muscle man here is a philosophy major, if you can believe it. I'm in the School of Engineering at UMass."

"Really? What branch of engineering?"

"Electrical," Chill answered for him. "Skip's a real live wire."

"Shocking, isn't it?" Guy put in.

"Yes."

Sarah wasn't trying to be funny. She had no clear notion of what electrical engineers did, but she was reasonably sure anybody with that much high-voltage erudition should be able to fiddle a home burglar-alarm system. After that, she couldn't think of much to say until they got back to the auditorium.

"We won't come in with you, if you don't mind," said Guy. "We've all got stuff to do. See you tomorrow night?"

"I'll be here. Thanks for the supper. It was fun." Some of it.

"Our pleasure."

They were off. Sarah glanced at her watch and realized she wouldn't have time for the quick freshening-up she'd hoped she could squeeze in before the dress rehearsal. In fact, she was barely inside the stage door when Heatherstone delivered Aunt Emma.

Mrs. Kelling was not yet in costume, of course, but she did have on her grandest wig and a vast amount of jewelry: yards and yards of jet interspersed with cameos ranging in size from one to four inches across.

"Stand there and let me drink you in," Sarah cried. "Where in the name of all that's good and holy did you find that incredible parure?"

"Like it?"

Emma waggled her head to start the blobbed and tasseled eardrops swinging, and revolved slowly so her niece could get the full effect of the many-tiered choker, the bracelets, the high-backed combs, the lavishly draped lavaliere, the rings, the stickpins, and the mammoth cameo brooch depicting Paris with Venus, Juno, and Athene, the golden apple of discord, and the apple tree it presumably came from.

"I picked it up at the antique exchange. It seemed just the thing for Lady Sangazure. When I die, I'm going to will it to Cousin Mabel."

"What a beautiful thought! Come on, I'll help you into your bustle."

They'd done a couple of trial runs earlier in the week. Sarah was able to confront the bulky accouterment with no real sense of panic. Things might have decayed in the bustlemaking trade, as Patrick Barrington* erst so melodiously averred, but the bustle with which Emma Kelling proposed to enhance her role was still going strong. Clearly this particular bustlemaker had built bustles with a will then, he'd built bustles with a wit. For all Sarah knew, he'd built bustles as a Yankee hustles, simply for the love of it.

This was no modified sofa pillow with a mere tape to tie around the waist, but a complicated structure of wire and whalebone, shaped generally on the principle of the Appalachian egg basket and scaled to fit a lady of already generous proportions. Sarah knew in her heart of hearts that she'd never have what it took to wear that bustle, steatopygia not being a

---

*I was a Bustlemaker Once, Girls; Patrick Barrington; Bradbury, Agnew & Co., Ltd., London (also *Punch*).

Kelling characteristic, but she yearned over it all the same. It was something merely to adjust the appurtenance over Aunt Emma's nethermost petticoat and snug in the waistband.

"There," she said, "does that feel comfortable?"

"Oddly enough, yes," Mrs. Kelling replied. "Have you got it fastened securely?"

"Not yet. Turn your back to the light, will you? I have to do these pesky hooks and eyes."

As she was bending over the bustle, trying to cope with the awkward fastenings, Sarah noticed something she could swear hadn't been there before. The tapes that held the wire to the whalebone now had printing on them: clumsy letters done with a smudgy felt-tipped pen. Reading from tape to tape, she made out the message, "Tomorrow is the day."

What was that supposed to mean? That tonight was just the dress rehearsal and tomorrow the real performance? Sarah thought not. Well, much as Aunt Emma hated having her feelings spared, Sarah was not going to tell her she was about to play Lady Sangazure with what was almost certainly another missive from Ernestina's kidnappers appended to her rear elevation. She picked up the voluminously befrilled awning affair that draped over the bustle before the top petticoat went on and lashed it in place before Emma could get a look at herself in the mirror.

Then came the rustling petticoat, then the purple taffeta gown, and more hooks and eyes and tiny cloth-covered buttons with fragile miniature loops they had to be coaxed through; then the panoply of cameos and jet, then the mauve satin bonnet bedecked with ostrich tips, artificial violets, and broad mauve satin ribbons that would be tied in a bow halfway up her left cheek after Emma had got her makeup on, for even Lady Sangazure had a touch of the flirt in her.

"Thank you, Sarah. I'll do my own face. You'd better run along and see what's doing out there."

It was high time she did. Sarah found three or four members of the chorus already clustered around the makeup table. She picked up a stick of bright orange greasepaint, sent up a silent orison to whatever deity might be in charge of painting actors' faces, and got to work. Her first attempt was passable, her second a little better. By the time she'd done three or four, she was feeling confident enough to start throwing in a few flourishes. She gave Dr. Daly rosy cheeks and a nose to match. She exaggerated Cousin Frederick's bushy eyebrows and Kelling nose to make him appear an even plainer old man than nature had intended.

Ridpath Wale was next in line, wearing a plain black suit with a high wing collar and a severe dark cravat. While Sarah was meditating her line of approach, wondering whether to emphasize the wizard or the businessman, he noticed a paperclip lying on the table and picked it up. A bit sheepishly, he then pulled a whole chain of them from his pocket and looped his latest find on the end.

"Can't help it," he confessed. "These are my worry beads. Something to fiddle with, you know. I tell myself you never know when a paper clip will come in handy."

"No," Sarah replied. "You don't, do you?"

She was thinking about those two paper clips she'd found pinning that other ransom note to the library screen, and about how the Sorcerer hadn't been needed at the rehearsal until well after she'd managed to get loose from the potting shed.

"Are you going to give me a sinister black mustache?" Ridpath asked as she began smearing greasepaint on his chin.

"I hardly think that's necessary," she told him. "I find you quite sinister enough, just as you are."

Chapter 11

Dame Partlett was Sarah's next customer, neat and far from gaudy in her ankle-length brown dress set off by a plain white apron, kerchief, and ruffled cap. Martha was looking downcast and sober as befitted her role of pew opener. It was a trifle early for her to start acting, Sarah thought.

Cousin Frederick, who was still hanging around the makeup table either for moral support or for want of anything better to do, noticed also.

"Why so glum, Martha?"

"Hello, Fred. Don't ask me to talk just now. I'm getting bedizened."

"You look a damn sight better without that glop on your face. Watch it, Sarah. You're making her look old."

"I am old," said Martha, keeping her lips stiff so as not to discommode Sarah.

That didn't go down with Frederick. "You old? Balderdash! You're a damn sight younger than I am."

"No young giddy, thoughtless maiden full of graces, airs, and jeers; but a sober widow laden with the weight of fifty years."

It was Martha's number, but Sarah was the singer. She'd meant to lighten the mood of the moment. She'd have done better to keep her mouth shut. Why remind Martha Tippleton that she'd soon be having to sing those lyrics to her own husband while the cast stood around trying to put a brave face on so

111

obvious a misalliance as Sir Marmaduke's getting himself plighted to a member of the servant class? Whatever had possessed Aunt Emma to permit so tasteless a piece of casting?

The situation might be merely amusing if Jack Tippleton could have refrained from making an ass of himself over a younger woman, but Aunt Emma ought to have known he couldn't. There he came now, out of the men's dressing room. He'd done his own makeup, getting himself up to look at least twenty years younger than his part called for.

And there was Gillian Bruges darting up to drop him a curtsy, winsome as all get-out in a costume like Martha's but with perky white ruffles on the kerchief and apron, and saucy white polka dots on the demure brown dress. She had chestnut-colored ribbons on her cap, and chestnut brown false ringlets peeping out from under its ruffle. If Uncle Jem were here, he'd be calling her a fetching minx.

Sarah could think of a few other things to call her. Didn't Gillian know better than to carry on her flirtation, even if it was nothing more than that, directly under Martha Tippleton's nose? Or was that part of the fun? It was a matter of deep personal satisfaction to Sarah when Aunt Emma sailed out with her bustle a-rustle and put the superannuated swain in his place.

"For the love of heaven, Jack, what have you done to your face? You're supposed to be a respectable English country squire, not a gone-to-seed Riviera gigolo. Sarah, fix him up quickly. Ready, Martha? They're starting the overture. Come along, Gillian. I've never held a curtain for anybody yet, and I don't intend to start with you."

"Break a leg, Mummy." That was the lovely Aline, running to give Martha a going-onstage hug. "You look sweet enough to eat in that cap. Doesn't she, Daddy?"

Jack made some kind of noise. That might have been the best he could do. Sarah had slathered him with cold cream and was scrubbing away the Don Juan makeup without regard to his finer feelings. Jenicot put on a gallant grin and tried again.

"Isn't it fun that we're all three doing a show together? The family that sings together clings together. How about that, Daddy?"

Emma Kelling gave the struggling girl a quick pat. "Yes, Jenny dear, it's lovely. Go call Parker and Sebastian. I want them ready and waiting in the wings before Gillian finishes her number. Honestly, Jack, at your age, one might have thought you'd know better."

It was not an auspicious beginning. Sarah hoped the senior citizens weren't in for too big a letdown. She reckoned without Aunt Emma.

Precisely what Emma Kelling said or did backstage to make Jack Tippleton quit making a fool of himself, to turn Gillian Bruges into a model of propriety, to sort out Cousin Frederick's two left feet and put some starch into Martha Tippleton's wilting backbone, Sarah never knew. Her aunt had ordered her out front, to monitor the performance from the audience's point of view.

Whatever it was, it worked. There were rough spots, naturally, since this was the first opportunity the performers had had to run through the entire show from the auditorium stage. On the whole, though, the dress rehearsal went as well as any amateur group could expect, and no doubt a good deal smoother than most.

The star of the evening, to everyone else's astonishment and his own dismay, was Frederick Kelling. The instant he set foot onstage, the children from his school began applauding. Those whose infirmities didn't allow them to clap managed to cheer, scream, pound the floor with their crutches, or beep the horns on their wheelchairs.

Sarah didn't mind their noise a bit. At least it was keeping her awake. Last night had caught up with her, even the coffee she'd had with the boys wasn't helping. She kept dropping off and waking up with a jerk. It was a good thing she'd picked a seat well toward the rear so the cast and the rest of the small audience couldn't see her disgracing herself.

Her makeups weren't bad, Sarah decided. She'd done a better job than some of the cast who'd put on their own, Jenicot Tippleton in particular. Jenny's voice might not be up to Gillian's, but she was far and away the prettier of the two. Onstage tonight, though, she wasn't coming off anywhere near so well. Gillian must have had more stage experience than she'd admitted to, or else she was an awfully quick learner. As a further else, Jenicot's makeup might have been all right to start with, and she'd messed it up.

By crying, Sarah decided after she'd slipped half-way down the aisle to get a better look. The tears wouldn't have been from a premature case of first-night nerves, either. There'd been that anguished little scene at the makeup table: Jenicot trying to wheedle her father into helping her pretend they were a loving, united family; Martha either in despair or in some mood close enough to it as made no difference; Jack paying no attention to either one of them.

Could Jenicot be imagining Jack was more serious about Gillian Bruges than he'd been about any of his previous infatuations? Sarah could have told her differently. She'd received enough sighs and glances herself during the past couple of days to convince her that Jack was willing to bestow his attentions elsewhere at the drop of an eyelash. She didn't think Gillian could have any real illusions about the duration of the romance, either, and she didn't think Gillian cared much one way or the other. Jack was just somebody who liked to play the same kind of game Gillian did. It would be over soon. After having seen so many other sexy soubrettes come and go, didn't Martha and Jenicot realize this one would dance herself offstage too?

There was such a thing as reaching the saturation point. Perhaps Martha had simply taken all she could stand. Sarah could remember altogether too well how her own first husband had finally given way under the load he'd been carrying for perhaps as many years as Martha had been married to Jack. Alexander had behaved much like Martha before his breakdown, going through the motions politely, mechanically, sinking into total apathy once he'd forced himself to the limit. He'd frightened Sarah then. Was Martha frightening Jenicot now?

Anyway, Jack Tippleton's affair was not Sarah's. Her business right now was with Aunt Emma's stolen Romney and whether Charlie Daventer's death had anything to do with it. Whatever ailed Martha Tippleton must be something quite apart. Mustn't it?

Martha Tippleton didn't have any money of her own. Sarah had gleaned that bit of information from Cousin Frederick, and Frederick had got it straight from Cousin Dolph. Suppose Martha needed cash in a hurry?

Suppose she did? Swiping Ernestina would be about the nuttiest way to get it one could possibly imagine. To begin with, she could never possibly have managed without help. Whom could she get for a job like that? Martha would hardly involve her own daughter. Besides, she was one of Emma Kelling's closest friends.

And what if she was? Best friends were the easiest people in the world to steal from, just because they never dreamed their best friends would betray them. Having easy access to Emma's treasures, though, Martha would also have Emma's pocketbook at her disposal. Everybody knew how readily Emma Kelling would come to the rescue in time of need. Was there some kind of twisted ethic that made it more honorable to steal than to beg?

Sarah wished she knew more about burglar alarms. She tried to remember some of the things Max had told her, but all she could think of was Max. He'd come home, she was running to meet him. He'd brought her the Swan of Tuonela for a souvenir. The swan was making a dreadful racket.

But not a swanlike racket. Good heavens, those were the children screaming again. Cousin Frederick was back onstage for the finale. She'd slept through almost the whole show. Sarah tried to pull herself together, hoping her aunt hadn't missed her. During the intermission, those backstage would, she hoped, have thought she was busy with the youngsters and oldsters out front. No doubt she ought to have been, though they all looked pretty well able to take care of themselves. She tried to concentrate on what was left of the performance.

The spell was broken. The ill-matched couples had got themselves sorted out. Frederick was paired off with Martha and looking pleased as Punch about it. On the other hand, he might just be relieved to have survived the performance. Anyway, Martha had brightened up, too, as she linked arms with him and did a discreet jig step. Alexis and Aline were together again, Lady Sangazure had Sir Marmaduke firmly in tow. Constance Partlett had been united to the rosy-nosed Dr. Daly and the Sorcerer had been banished with his evil spirits to the infernal regions under the trapdoor at the rear of the stage.

Sarah had always thought this punishment a rank injustice, considering it had been Alexis who'd talked the Sorcerer into preparing his mischievous potion in the first place. Alexis was being self-righteous and triumphant as befitted a member of the aristocracy who'd got what he wanted and need not concern himself with the tribulations of the working class. Parker was carrying it off with panache too; he could act as well as sing. Sarah found it interesting that a nice, diffident boy like Parker Pence could project so much arrogance. Maybe the acting was in the diffidence, but why would he do that?

Never mind Parker, she'd better attend to her business. Should she go backstage now, or wait for the end? Sarah decided to wait, she liked the rollicking bun number. She liked them all, for that matter. How could she have slept through so much of the performance?

Max could drop off at odd times for quick naps, but she herself had never caught the knack. Sarah wondered for a second whether Guy might have slipped something into her peppermint ice cream, then decided she was simply tired. How Aunt Emma had kept up the pace year after year was more than Sarah could imagine. On the other hand, Aunt Emma hadn't been up half the night trying to help Cousin Frederick investigate her old sweetheart's murder.

Horrible reminder: Sarah had promised Sergeant Formsby she'd call on Cousin Mabel. It would be an agonizing exercise in futility, but a promise was a promise. Besides, if there was anything that could possibly be told to the detriment of anybody in the cast, she could absolutely count on Cousin Mabel to tell it.

There, the finale was concluded, and nicely too. The curtains closed, then reopened to show the entire cast, chorus and principals. No, not the entire cast. The Sorcerer was missing and Sarah could see that the smile on Lady Sangazure's face was forced. She left her seat and ran around backstage.

They were just coming off. The first person she met was Emma Kelling, definitely unsmiling now. "Where's Ridpath?" she panted.

"I don't know," said her aunt. "He was supposed to pop up through the trapdoor. Go see if it's stuck, quickly while we start our individual bows."

Sarah knew the trapdoor led down by a few ladderlike steps into the T-shaped funnel through which the musicians entered the orchestra pit. With openings at both sides of the stage as well as the one into the pit, it seemed impossible he'd got trapped down there. She practically leaped the short staircase that led down from the wings and entered the tunnel.

"Ridpath, are you here?"

"Yes! For God's sake, help me."

"What happened? Did you fall?"

"I damned near killed myself. Look."

Sarah gaped. "What's wrong with the stairs?" The top one was hanging askew.

"A screw must have come out," Ridpath told her. "It looked all right when I stepped down, but it pivoted and threw me when I put my weight on it."

"Oh, Ridpath! Can you walk?"

"I didn't dare try. Help me, will you?"

With the orchestra blaring the finale outside, his groans were, Sarah hoped, drowned. She got him to his feet and made him take a step or two. As far as she could tell, it was merely a sprain.

"My trousers are the worst casualty," Ridpath admitted. "They're split from stem to gudgeon. I can't possibly take a curtain call."

"You must. Those children out front would think you'd really died. Come on."

She hustled him back upstairs as fast as she dared, parked him in the wings, and grabbed three of the spectres' thrown-off shrouds.

"Here, wrap this around you. Come here, you two."

There were a couple of hearty-looking young men

working the lights and ropes. Sarah draped them hastily in the phosphorescent gauze, made them hoist Ridpath between them, handed him one of the artificial calla lilies Aline had carried in the betrothal scene, and stood by to dim the stage lights. As Emma came offstage with blood in her eye, the Sorcerer gave her a gallant wave of his lily and let himself be escorted onstage by his ghostly bearers. Even Cousin Frederick hadn't got a bigger ovation.

When he came off, Emma hugged him. "Ridpath, you rogue! That was magnificent. We'll do it tomorrow. However did you get the idea?"

"Needs must when the devil drives," he told her. "Thank you, my stalwart men-at-arms. Tomorrow night I'll get a couple of my creditors to help. They've been carrying me for years. Just an old joke I've always wanted to work off on somebody, Emma dear; you needn't offer me a loan. But you had better get those steps under the trapdoor seen to."

"What do you mean? I tested them myself, this afternoon. Ridpath, you didn't slip and fall?"

"Not precisely, no. It's all right, Emma. Let's not make a fuss."

"A screw came loose and he twisted his ankle," Sarah put in quickly. "Stick it in a bucket of cold water as soon as you've changed, Ridpath. Do you want to get out of your costume before you hold the cast conference, Aunt Emma?"

"Yes, why don't we all? Then we can go straight home afterward without having to bother. Hang your costumes up carefully everyone, please, so we shan't have to press them again tomorrow. Back onstage as soon as you're dressed. We don't want to be here all night."

A few people were asking Ridpath for details of his accident, but Emma shushed them up and shooed them toward the dressing rooms like an elderly goose girl herding her flock. Sarah was glad they were getting away from the wings. With so many clustered in such a narrow space, the press of bodies and the smell of greasepaint was getting on her nerves.

"Am I supposed to take their makeup off for them?" she asked her aunt.

"Only if they scream for help. I myself shall start screaming if I don't get out of this straitjacket pretty soon. I'd no idea a bustle was such a responsibility."

"What's that you've got sticking to your rumble seat, Emma?" Ridpath Wale asked her. "I don't recall having seen it when you came offstage."

"What are you talking about?" Emma reached around behind her, as far back as she could manage. "How odd. Sarah, what am I touching?"

"Somebody's idea of a joke, I think." Sarah could feel a sudden dryness in her mouth. "It's a note, skewered on with an old-fashioned hatpin. I expect it says 'Kick Me,' or something equally brilliant. No, Ridpath, you scoot on ahead and do something about your ankle. I'll take care of the note. If the pin should catch, that old taffeta might split."

She was not about to let him find out what that alleged hatpin really was. She'd recognized it at first glance. That had been one of Uncle Bed's little games with her, letting her trace the spiraled pattern with one finger and teaching her to say, "Ka-nurled ka-nob." He'd never let her handle the paper knife to which the knurled knob was attached, though, because little girls must never handle dangerously sharp objects for fear of cutting their tender hands.

Sarah waited until Ridpath had limped behind one of the folding screens from which dressing rooms had been improvised before she pulled the knife out of the bustle. She waited again until she and her aunt were shut into the only bona fide separate dressing room, the one Emma Kelling always reserved for herself, before she opened the note that had been skewered to the cloth.

This one was typed. TWO DOWN, ONE TO GO. PAY UP OR YOU LOSE MORE THAN YOUR PAINTING.

Emma stared at the paper. "Sarah, whatever can this mean?"

"Do you honestly want to discuss it now?"

"Sarah Kelling, if you know something I don't, you tell it to me this instant."

"All right, then. I'm afraid it means Ridpath Wale wasn't supposed to survive that fall just now. Cousin Frederick and I don't believe Charlie Daventer's death was any accident, either."

"Help me out of my costume."

Sarah obeyed, unfastening hooks and eyes and tiny buttons as she talked. Emma stood there in her whalebone and petticoats, stoic as the Roman soldier at Pompeii ignoring the molten lava as it flowed around his legs. When Sarah paused for breath, all she said was, "Go on."

Sarah went on until she had nothing left to tell. At the end, Emma's comment was, "Don't let my dress drop to the floor unless you're prepared to press it. Get up on that chair and pull it over my head. Make sure the legs are on tight."

Chapter 12

This single-minded concentration on the project at hand was a trifle scary. What would happen once the show was behind them and Emma Kelling turned her full attention to tracking down her old cavalier's murderer, as she was sure to do? Sarah was wondering about that as she undid the bustle's complicated moorings and helped her aunt into a pink *plissé* kimono so she could get her stage makeup off without messing her clothes.

Now that the cat was out of the bag, Sarah showed Emma the other message printed on the bustle tapes. Reading it off, she remarked on what a trivial bit of nonsense it sounded in comparison to the typewritten threat with the dagger driven through it.

Emma thought so too. "Rather a waste of powder and shot, wouldn't you say?"

Sarah nodded. "Two notes on the same bustle do seem a bit much. And they're so different. Almost as if—"

She was interrupted by a knock on the door and Jenicot's voice calling, "Mrs. Kelling?"

"Yes, Jenny?"

The door opened and the girl's head appeared. "Mother sent me to tell you everybody's ready. Oh, sorry. I didn't realize you weren't dressed."

She pulled back and shut the door in a hurry. Sarah was amused.

"Aunt Emma, I hadn't realized you're such a martinet. That girl looked positively scared to death."

"They know I don't like to be bothered in my dressing room," Emma mumbled through a faceful of cold cream. "Reach me that box of tissues, will you?"

That ended any talk about the two notes. Emma had to be hurried into her clothes and rushed onstage for the postoperative consultation, as Sebastian Frostedd insisted on calling it. Sarah was relieved he didn't say postmortem. She discovered she was not only expected to attend with the rest, but to make intelligent observations based on what she was supposed to have noticed from the front of the house. These took a bit of doing, since she had a natural reluctance to let the cast know how much of their performance she'd slept through.

She did manage to dredge up a suggestion that Gillian refrain from maneuvering herself upstage and thus forcing Dame Partlett to turn her back to the audience. That gave her a small and transient satisfaction and earned her a glance of approval from Frederick, who appeared to have taken Martha under his wing along with his schoolful of handicapped children. She dug up a few more scraps of corroborative detail to add verisimilitude to an otherwise unconvincing report, added quite truthfully that the audience had loved the show, and backed herself off with a compliment on Frederick's stellar performance that embarrassed him a good deal.

It was interesting to watch Emma Kelling take the show apart and put it back together again without hurting anybody's feelings, though Sarah was awfully glad when she'd finished. It wasn't until they'd shut off the stage lights and were going out to the parking lot that Emma showed any sign of nerves.

"Frederick, I wish you'd come back and spend the night with us."

"What for?" was his gracious reply.

"Because we need you. Please, Frederick."

It wasn't like Emma to beg a personal favor. Frederick gave her a sharp glance, then nodded. "I'll have to stop by my flat and pick up my razor."

"You can use Bed's."

"Rather have my own," he grumbled. "What about pajamas?"

"I have some of Young Bed's old ones that will fit you. I keep them for the grandchildren when they sleep over. Don't fuss, Fred. You'll be perfectly comfortable."

She strong-armed him into Sarah's car, Heatherstone having been sent home ages ago to rest up for tomorrow. "There, now we can talk. Sarah's told me the dreadful news about poor Charlie. You do believe it, Fred?"

"Would I go around shooting off my mouth to the police if I didn't? What kind of fool do you take me for?"

"Oh Fred, don't be a prune. You know I trust your judgment as I would my own. It's just that I can't quite take it in. What are we going to do?"

"Wait and see what the police turn up, I suppose. That Sergeant Formsby didn't strike me as any dumbbell."

"All right, we'll do that. But what about the funeral? You and I are Charlie's executors, aren't we?"

"We are. I've already been to see Muffenson. The will's perfectly straightforward, thank God. He's left you his furniture, which you don't need, and me his books, which I'll be glad to have. His money goes to the school, which was damned decent of him, except for a few small bequests. A thousand to the BSO, another thousand to the Horticultural Society in memory of his mother, that sort of thing. We can go over it in detail when the time comes to cough up. As for the funeral, he didn't want one."

"Did he actually put that in the will? I must say it doesn't surprise me. Charlie used to say that for all he cared, we could simply wrap him in brown paper and mail him out of town. Oh Fred, I'm going to miss him!"

"Now Emma, don't go turning on the waterworks. It's late and I'm tired, dammit. Charlie stipulated that he's to be cremated with no fuss nor feathers and his ashes scattered over your rose garden in the pious hope they'll be of some small benefit to the local ecology."

"Oh dear. I honestly don't think I could bear having little bits of Charlie turning up among the mulch."

"Humbug. What's the sense of being squeamish? If Charlie didn't mind, why the hell should you? Funny how people get these sentimental notions about their outworn carcasses, isn't it? Do you recall when Joe Pomfret died? He wanted his ashes scattered over Boston Harbor. This was back before they'd started trying to clean it up, and apparently Joe hadn't gone to check it out before he made his will.

"Well, anyway, Bed and I went down to T Wharf and hired some old gaffer to take us out in a damned stinking tub of a charter boat. We spent the whole day cruising around trying to find a spot that didn't have any oil slicks or raw sewage floating around. Finally we gave up and put into the wharf again, half frozen and still lugging that blasted box of ashes.

"So Bed said the hell with it, let's go have a drink. He and I went back to South Station, bellied up to the oyster bar, and ordered a few martinis and an oyster stew. Then we walked back to the Fort Point Bridge and dumped Joe over the railing on the outgoing tide. By then it was too dark to see what he landed on, and we were too drunk to care."

Frederick snickered at this vignette from the past, then sobered. "None of that folderol when I go, Emma.

I want a cheap pine box and I want to be planted in the family plot next to Mother and Father and Lucy. Why cheat the worms out of a supper just because it's not stylish to park your bones next to the old folks any more?"

"Yes, Frederick. I'll see to it, assuming you don't get to bury me first. And naturally we'll do as Charlie wanted. Have you fixed things with the undertaker?"

"I have. We're due at the crematorium tomorrow morning. Ten o'clock sharp."

"So soon?" Emma sighed. "All right, then. You and me, and Sarah if she wants to come, though I can't imagine why she would. Who else?"

"What about the Tippletons? Charlie always thought Jack was an awful fool, but he liked Martha."

"Just Martha, then. Actually I don't suppose we need ask anybody at all, merely to go over there and stand around the furnace, if that's what one does. It would be much nicer to have a little memorial gathering at the house, perhaps on Sunday afternoon when we're all rested up from the show. Drinks and little sandwiches, you know, and the orchestra playing some of the songs we used to dance to. We'll ask people to bring their old snapshots of Charlie, and show them around and chat about the happy times. Oh, Fred!"

"Now, Emma. I'm going to miss the old buzzard as much as you are, but you don't catch me giving way. Come on, chin up. Stiff upper lip."

"Stiff upper horsefeathers!" Emma sniffed a few times, made vigorous use of her handkerchief, and straightened her spine. "Frederick, what makes you so sure Charlie was murdered?"

Kellings never did have much patience with namby-pamby notions about finer feelings. Frederick told. Emma nodded.

"Yes, of course. I'd have found that out for myself if you hadn't beaten me to it. Charlie told me about his little arrangement one day when I'd asked him how he was managing you know, as one naturally would. We had a good chuckle over the family heirloom. He wants it to go to the Massachusetts Historical Society, by the way. Polished first, I suppose."

"I know. That's in the will too. There aren't any Daventers left except that third cousin of his, and I don't have to tell you what Charlie thought of Lemuel. He's left him two dollars to buy a girlie magazine."

"Frederick, he didn't." Emma was laughing and choking at the same time.

"It's right down there in black and white. Blast it, Emma, you might as well go ahead and bawl if it'll make you feel any better."

"Later," said Emma Kelling. "Right now I'm trying to remember where I put those pajamas."

Chapter 13

If anything else happened that night, Sarah didn't know about it. By the time they'd shared a jug of Slepe-o-tite and got Frederick bedded down in Young Bed's old room, she was quite ready to resume the slumber she'd begun at the rehearsal.

She woke early, though, noted it was going to be a fine day for the show, and felt an urge to be up and doing. Then Sarah remembered this was also her day to visit Cousin Mabel and wished she hadn't waked up at all. Even Henry Wadsworth Longfellow wouldn't have much heart for that particular fate, she brooded as she brushed her teeth.

However, as Ridpath Wale had so aptly put it last night, needs must when the devil drives. She hoped that ankle of his wasn't going to give him too much trouble. It might be possible for the Sorcerer to play his part on crutches, but Sarah couldn't see where they'd add much to the dramatic effect.

That unscrewed step down from the trapdoor bothered her very much. It hadn't caused Ridpath a very long fall. Even if he'd taken a headlong spill, he might have got out of it with nothing worse than a mild concussion or a broken collarbone. On the other hand, he might have broken his neck. From the tenor of the note stabbed into Aunt Emma's bustle, he'd been meant to.

The note must have been written well before Ridpath was hurt. There was no typewriter backstage, or anywhere else in the auditorium that Sarah could recall, and she'd covered most of it during the past couple of days, on one or another of her aunt's commissions. She wondered if by any chance it might turn out to have been typed on the machine downstairs in the library, at the same time the paper knife was taken. It was strange about that knife. Surely whoever took it must have known Emma would recognize her own property. It must have been taken sometime yesterday. Sarah was pretty sure she'd noticed the paper knife on Uncle Bed's desk Wednesday when she'd been checking for signs of a break-in, just before she saw the note on the screen.

And why couldn't the knife have been taken soon afterward, maybe while she was trapped in the potting shed? She hadn't gone back to the library. The entire ensemble—cast, chorus, and orchestra—was in the house then. Aunt Emma had been busy with the rehearsal and the Heatherstones with the buffet. To accomplish all that without being missed from the rehearsal would have taken some pretty fancy footwork, though. It seemed more and more that at least two people must be involved in this wicked business. Now it looked as if they must all be connected in one way or another with the show, and that seemed hard to swallow.

Unless it was the Tippletons. Jenicot's notion of togetherness, perhaps; the family that robbed together hobnobbed together. That meant Jack's infatuation with Gillian Bruges, his indifference to his wife and daughter were feigned. Sarah didn't believe that for one second. Jack was a randy old rooster, Martha a well-trodden doormat, and Jenicot a daughter in distress, looking for a happy ending she wasn't likely to find unless she managed to create a separate one for herself.

Of course if one got to thinking of families, some of the people Sarah had assumed were out of it might as well be counted in. Maybe Parker Pence's father had been masterminding from behind the kettledrums while his son did the dirty work and Mrs. Pence carried the stolen paper knife away in her flute case. Stranger things had happened, but surely not in Emma Kelling's drawing room. Would respectable parents embroil their children in such nefarious doings? Would sensible parents trust their children to do as they were told and keep their mouths shut about it? Not that Parker could be called a child, Sarah supposed, but he seemed awfully callow to her.

And what if he was? Guy Mannering didn't strike Sarah as any master of guile either, but he did have those two friends taking stiff college majors. A philosopher to work out a plan, an electrical engineer to handle the technicalities, Guy himself the scene painter with a glorious excuse to invade Emma's house and learn the lie of the land; they'd make an effective team. They'd said they weren't coming back to the rehearsal, but that didn't mean they hadn't done so. Or that one of them hadn't.

Skip, she thought, the skinny one who could curl himself up in impossible places. He could have secreted the paper knife while they were putting up the scenery, watched his chance to drive it into the bustle while Aunt Emma was passing by with that single mind of hers fixed on the performance, and made his escape perhaps during the finale while everybody was onstage. Such a stunt would appeal to that crude schoolboy sense of humor she'd been treated to a dose of when they went out to supper.

Well, it was one more thing to think about. Sarah climbed out of the shower and toweled herself dry. No old pants and jersey today. Cousin Mabel would take it as a personal affront if she didn't show up dressed to the teeth. Mabel would also take it as a personal affront if she did, but that couldn't be helped. Her natural linen skirt and blazer, with a blue silk blouse, would be a reasonable compromise. If Aunt Emma had some chore for her, she could borrow a smock.

It was almost a shock, after the all-out involvement of the past week, to realize that after tonight everything would be over. After so much preparation, one might have thought they'd do three or four performances, but perhaps that was part of Emma Kelling's mystique. By making her operettas once-and-never-again events, she made everybody and his grandfather feel they absolutely had to be there. The auditorium would be packed to the eaves tonight. It always was. She buttoned her blouse and went downstairs.

Heatherstone was just starting upstairs with the tea tray. Sarah took the cup he'd meant for her and carried it out to the sun parlor. The room was still chilly, but the sun was up. It would be warm soon. Sarah hoped the sun would shine again Sunday for Charlie's memorial gathering.

Not that the occasion would be a dreary one in any event; there'd be too many Kellings around. Kellings, by and large, adored a funeral. This one wouldn't be up to standard without the guest of honor present, but they'd make the most of what they could get. Dolph would pontificate, Uncle Theodore would quaver, "So young to be taken," and Aunt Priscilla insist, "A blessed release." Aunt Appie would be crushed with grief over not getting to pay her personal last respects to the dear departed, which to her would have meant standing over the open coffin, shedding tears and hairpins all over the undertaker's painstaking handiwork. Cousin Theonia, though only an in-law, would enter into the spirit of the occasion, cooing like the mourning dove *Zenaidura macroura*, "Such a loss to his dear ones."

His dear ones in Charlie's case would be primarily Emma and Frederick, as far as Sarah knew; unless

the detested Lemuel showed up, in which case Aunt
Appie would doubtless be good-natured enough to
cry over him. Cousin Frederick must have sent him
a telegram from a sense of executorial duty, but Sarah
could imagine what he'd put in it. CHARLES DEAD.
DON'T COME. NOTHING IN IT FOR YOU.

The hot tea tasted good, but it was making her
hungry. Sarah went out to see whether Mrs. Heatherstone had started breakfast yet, found her frying
pancakes, and helped herself to one hot from the pan.
Pancakes with the real maple syrup they'd surely
get at Emma's were lovely, but Sarah liked them
even better rolled up with butter and jam inside.

"Here, put on this apron so you won't spot your
pretty blouse," Mrs. Heatherstone scolded. "And stay
in the kitchen to eat that. I won't have you tracking
melted butter all over the house."

"Yes, Mrs. Heatherstone," Sarah replied meekly,
and sat down like a good child with a plate and
napkin. She'd be going home tomorrow evening, most
likely, then she could eat where she chose. Max was
a great one for having picnic meals wherever he took
the notion, and she'd picked up the habit from him.
What was he eating now, she wondered, and where,
and how soon would he get back to Boston?

Sarah realized she was having mixed feelings
about Max's homecoming. She ached to have him
back, but she dreaded having to plunge him into yet
another family crisis. Things had been the same when
Alexander was alive, everybody expecting Sarah's
husband to pull them out of the soup, leaving him
no time for Sarah. She sighed and rolled herself another pancake.

"You keep that up, young woman, and you won't
have any appetite for breakfast." Mrs. Heatherstone
couldn't seem to remember Sarah was grown up and
twice married. "Now go along and set the table for
me, like a good girl."

Sarah obeyed as she always had. She couldn't quite recall the first time her parents had parked her at Aunt Emma's. The last had been when she was ten, the time her parents had gone on an extended tour of Europe. That must have been right after her mother had learned she was terminally ill and made up her mind to do all the things she'd been putting off while she was still able. Nobody had bothered to tell Sarah that. She hadn't minded being left behind; to go would have meant having to memorize too many guidebooks in order to get the maximum benefit from her cultural experience. Here in Pleasaunce, she'd been allowed to read Uncle Bed's mystery novels instead.

They'd been innocent enough, she realized now; no sex, less violence than she'd found in her fairy stories, lots of earnest cogitation often based on remarkably silly premises. If it weren't for the unrefined nature of Cousin Frederick's clue, the current Kelling predicament might have fitted comfortably into one of Uncle Bed's genteel thrillers: a valuable family portrait gone, a murder made to look like the commonest sort of accident; a perfect setup for Miss Maud Silver to take off her second-best hat, pin on her bog-oak brooch, sit down with her knitting, and unravel the mystery.

But how many mysteries were there? Was it sensible to lump Charlie's death in with Ernestina's disappearance just because they'd happened on the same night? And because Charlie'd been in on the discussion about how much Ernestina might be worth on today's stolen art market? And because that last and nastiest note had said, "Two down, one to go"?

What about those notes, anyway? What was the point of all those vague menaces and no instructions about forking over the money? What sort of game did these crooks think they were playing?

Maybe they weren't real crooks. Maybe Four-

Square Jane was back on the job. Sarah couldn't help smiling at that notion as she arranged silver and napkins on the pale green linen place mats. She'd discovered Four-Square Jane here in Uncle Bed's library that summer when she was ten. Jane had been one of those emancipated ladies of early crime fiction, not a detective but a female Robin Hood who stole from the stingy rich to give to the worthy poor.

In one adventure Jane had abstracted a huge masterpiece from a rich man's gallery under seemingly impossible conditions and forced its flinthearted owner, by way of ransom, to send a large donation to a philanthropy he'd been holding out on. Once the check was cashed, she dropped him a note telling him to pull down his window blind. There was the treasured painting, cut out of its frame, pinned to the cloth, and simply rolled up out of sight.

She'd told Max the story not long ago. He'd hit the ceiling. In the first place, he'd pointed out, Jane would have marred the painting by cutting away the edge, and ruined the goddamn finish by cracking it all to hell when she rolled up the goddamn blind. In the third, the extra thickness of canvas would have caused the blind to bulk up so much that the owner would have had to be blind himself not to notice. In the fourth place, Jane wouldn't have been able to reach the painting in the first place. If the owner was such a tasteless clod as he was made out to be, he'd have skied the painting in the tasteless fashion of the day, hanging it up close to the ceiling. That would have been at least fourteen feet high and unreachable except by a long wooden ladder which Jane would have had one hell of a time tucking into her bloomers.

Max would never make a mystery fan. He was too unwilling to suspend logic in the interest of a good yarn. He did believe in playing one's hunches, though, and here was a point to consider. Would Sarah have thought of Four-Square Jane just now if Jane hadn't been trying to tell her something? Suppose the reason she couldn't figure out how the painting had been taken from the house was that in fact it hadn't. All right then, if it was still here, where was it?

Not rolled up in a window blind, surely. Not pinned behind a drapery, either, because Heatherstone would have noticed. Not cut out of its stretcher, thank goodness, or surely the remains would have been left in the frame.

Somewhere down cellar would be the obvious place, or rather the sort of un-obvious hideaway the thieves would have been looking for. There was stuff down there from generations back, even pieces Uncle Bed's great-grandparents hadn't been able to part with because who knew when they might come in handy? As children and grandchildren moved or married or set up apartments or redecorated their houses, things got shifted around, taken away, brought in, parked wherever a spot could be found. Even something the size of Ernestina could easily escape notice, especially nowadays when there were only the Heatherstones and part-time outside help to run Emma's complicated household. Nobody had time to keep tabs on nonessentials. Sarah folded the napkins into swimming swans the way Mrs. Heatherstone had taught her ages ago, set a pot of Aunt Emma's fairy primroses on the table to add a springtime note, and slipped down the back hall to the cellar.

Her first thought when she got down there was, "This could take forever." Her second was that things were neater than she'd expected and that none of them resembled a missing Romney. That didn't mean Ernestina wasn't there, naturally she'd be well camouflaged. Sarah poked around until she heard her aunt's voice demanding, "Isn't Sarah down yet?" and decided she'd better go up. She wouldn't say anything yet about her hunch. If she was right, Ernestina was safe enough. If she wasn't, this was hardly the time to start a hunt for an imaginary hare.

Cousin Frederick looked chipper enough after his night in Young Bed's outgrown pajamas. Looking at him and Emma together, both pretty much of an age, Sarah wondered why she called him cousin when Emma's sons, both a good deal older than she, called him uncle. In fact none of them could have said precisely how and in what degree Frederick was related to anybody. That was the way things tended to be among the Kellings. Relationships got so wildly intertwined that it didn't pay to be picky about accurate titles. Nobody cared anyway, except Cousin Mabel, who took her own spectacular brand of umbrage if any of the young folks dared to address her as aunt.

Mabel's invitation had been for lunch. Having a pretty good idea what that would amount to, Sarah decided she might as well fill up on pancakes and sausages. She didn't have to talk much; Emma and Frederick were absorbed in deciding whom they should ask to the memorial gathering tomorrow. Aunt Emma had come to the table equipped with her big address book, the slim gold pencil that hung from a chain around her neck and was as much a part of her as the diamond solitaires in her ears, and a fresh blue notebook.

At last Emma let the pencil swing back against her hand-embroidered gray silk blouse. "That's the lot, I think. Thank you, Fred. Sarah, if you're not keen on going to the crematorium, I wish you'd stay here and make some calls. Not that Saturday morning's the best time to catch people in, but I don't know what other time we'll have. We'll take the Buick, Heatherstone. Mrs. Heatherstone tells me she'd like to go, too. We can all stop on the way back and shop for groceries. I can't imagine what we're going to feed them all on such short notice, but we'll think of something. Too bad about Cousin Mabel, Sarah, but at least her having you to lunch gives us a golden excuse not to take her to the cremation with us. We'll have to ask her here tomorrow, I suppose, or I'll never hear the last of it. You give her the message, dear, will you? If I don't call her myself, perhaps she'll choose to be offended and stay away."

"No such luck," grunted Frederick. "You know what else to ask her, Sarah?" He was clearly weaseling out, as who wouldn't?

"If I can get a word in edgewise."

"What's Mabel supposed to know that I don't?" Emma demanded.

"Don't ask me," said Sarah. "It's just that her name came up night before last while Cousin Frederick and I were having our little chat with Sergeant Formsby. Somehow or other, he got the idea he ought to go over and give her the third degree."

"What a lovely idea."

"Aunt Emma, be serious. You know perfectly well what would happen if we'd ever let a policeman start asking Mabel about Charlie Daventer's private life. She'd have stirred up such a scandal you'd have had to call off the show. So I hurled myself into the breach and managed to persuade him that I'd have better luck worming things out of her than he would. Frankly, I don't think he needed much convincing."

"No, I don't suppose he would," Emma agreed, helping Frederick to the last sausage. "Mabel calls them to report a Peeping Tom on an average of six nights a week. Wishful thinking, pure and simple. What a pity her parents were too close-fisted to keep a gardener she could have run off with when she was a girl. Now then, Frederick, don't you think we ought to start girding our loins pretty soon?"

"My loins are as girded as they're going to get, Emma. It won't take us more than fifteen minutes at the outside to drive to the cemetery, so I'm going to sit here and digest my breakfast. Don't get one like this very often, I must say. If I weren't afraid of having my face slapped, I'd go out in the kitchen and kiss Mrs. Heatherstone."

"Why, Fred, what's come over you all of a sudden?"

"Keeping up my spirits, I suppose. No sense pulling a long face, is there? Charlie wouldn't want that. Anyway, I'll be joining him soon enough. I just hope I live long enough to get my hands on that swine who did him in. I've never thought of myself as a vindictive man but, by God, this is more than I can swallow."

Emma gave him a little pat on the shoulder. "I know, Frederick. I think what horrifies me most is the fear that his death may somehow have been connected with this stupid business about Ernestina. If I ever found out Charlie Daventer had lost his life over a few square feet of canvas off my own wall, I honestly believe I'd drop dead for shame."

"No you wouldn't. You'd be mad as hell, like me." Frederick pushed back his chair, stood up, and faced her squarely. "Emma, you don't for one split second think Charlie had any part in stealing your painting?"

"Frederick! How can you even dream of suggesting such a thing? My only thought was that since Charlie was here that night, he might possibly have caught on that something was in the wind. He was awfully clever at puzzles, you know, all those Double-Crostics and the crossword puzzles from the London *Times* when he could get hold of a free copy. But I don't see how that could have happened. Can you?"

"Emma, what's the sense in brooding over it before we have anything to go on? Where's your coat?"

Emma smoothed down her dark gray skirt and buttoned her jacket. She hadn't put on black for Charlie, Sarah noticed, probably because she'd had none to wear. She'd often said black was unflattering to women over forty. But she'd come as close as she could.

"I shan't want a coat, Fred. It should be warm enough in a crematorium, wouldn't you think? Heatherstone, please tell Mrs. Heatherstone we'll be ready by the time you bring the car around. Here's the list of names to call, Sarah. Just tell them what it's about, and four o'clock tomorrow afternoon. Oh, and the snapshots, if they have any. I'll just run upstairs and get my hat. Charlie always liked me in a hat."

Aunt Emma probably wanted a quiet sniffle, Sarah thought, as who wouldn't in her place? She carried the few remaining dishes out to the kitchen, told Mrs. Heatherstone not to bother with them now because Mrs. Kelling was putting her hat on, and went into the library. She might as well do her phoning where she could be most comfortable. It was going to be a long job.

Most of the people on Emma Kelling's list were either completely unknown to Sarah or the most casual of acquaintances. A few remembered her as the child who'd stayed with Emma and Bed when Walter's wife was in such a bad way and wasn't it a pity she went so young? They supposed Sarah must miss her mother dreadfully but didn't wait to be confirmed in their erroneous surmises. They were too eager to tell her how sad they felt about poor Charlie and how eagerly they were looking forward to *The Sorcerer*. Sarah cut them as short as she decently could, and went on dialing numbers.

She didn't catch many men. These must all have gone fishing or golfing, or be locked in their studies writing their memoirs, or whatever the males of Pleasaunce did on Saturday mornings. Fortunately, most of them had wives or daughters or housekeepers or possibly lady friends at home to take Sarah's

message. She'd managed to contact all but a few of
the names on Emma's list by the time she had to
bite the bullet and get ready for Mabel's luncheon.
And she still hadn't got back to searching the basement.

Sarah was dithering on the doorstep, wondering
if it was safe to leave the house unattended and
telling herself she was just stalling because she didn't
want to go, when Emma's car pulled up.

"Sarah, haven't you gone yet? I must say you look
stunning in that outfit. Mabel will be livid. Hop in,
dear. Heatherstone will drive you there."

"I was going in my own car," Sarah protested.

Emma waved her gloves in horror. "Sheer mad-
ness. If you do, Mabel will nag you into chauffeuring
her all over Pleasaunce and you'll be stuck for the
afternoon. Heatherstone will return punctually at
half-past one with a message that you're urgently
needed here. That will give you a safe out and Mabel
can revile me instead of you for breaking up her
party."

"I hadn't thought of that, not that I don't expect
to be reviled for something or other anyway. Where's
Cousin Frederick?"

"He asked us to drop him at Charlie's place. I do
hope he's not going morbid. All this detecting, you
know. I'm not sure it's healthy."

"I'll ask Max when he comes home. Here's your
list. The checks mean yes, the x's mean no, and the
question marks mean they're to call back. No mark,
no luck."

Sarah kissed her aunt and got into the car. She
didn't mind being driven, actually. She could use a
few minutes of doing nothing at all. Except, unfortunately, worry.

What did Frederick think he was looking for now?
Maybe just papers to do with Charlie's estate? She
kept forgetting he was an executor. Still, Sarah

wished he hadn't gone there by himself. That had been a funny remark of Aunt Emma's, "I'm not sure it's healthy." She wasn't usually tactless, unless one was trying to interfere with her current project. The worst of it was, she was right. Detecting could be the unhealthiest activity possible for a feisty old amateur who didn't know where the hazards might lie.

"Heatherstone," she said, "it mightn't be a bad idea for you to stop by on your way back and see if Cousin Frederick's changed his mind about lunching with my aunt."

"I was thinking of that myself, Sarah. To tell you the truth, I don't much like him being over there alone."

She might have known he'd see through her feeble wile. "It's just that all these nasty things have been happening. I wish my husband would come home."

"Better not say that in front of Miss Mabel. She'll have you divorced before you've finished your soup."

"What makes you think I'll get any soup? Ever stop to think what a privileged position you're in, Heatherstone?"

"Sorry if I've spoken out of turn," he replied somewhat huffily.

"I didn't mean that, silly. I meant about never having to eat lunch at Cousin Mabel's. She's always on a strict diet, you know, when she's the one who's paying for the groceries."

"Has to be, I suppose, on account of the way she eats when it's somebody else's grub. Mrs. Heatherstone always cooks extra when we're having Miss Mabel over, and I must say she never has to worry about what to do with the leftovers. Not that she minds doing it, you understand, and not that Mrs. Kelling would ever begrudge anybody a square meal regardless. Well, here we are, Sarah my girl. I better get out and hold the car door for you or she'll be down here reminding me I'm paid to wait on my betters."

"Not in front of me, she won't. Thanks, Heatherstone. I'll see you in a while, then. Just sit outside and honk the horn."

On that outrageous note, Sarah allowed herself to be helped from the car in grand style. She refrained from waving good-bye to the chauffeur and swept up the walk, her nose in the air and her heart in her boots.

Chapter 14

Back before restoring Victorian houses got to be fashionable, one of Emma Kelling's Boston friends had described Pleasaunce as a town where the architectural sins of the fathers were visited upon the children. There did seem to be a disproportionate number of leftover offspring rattling around inside their beporched and beturreted ancestral piles. Mabel Kelling was one of the rattlers.

Whereas Emma and Beddoes had, by judicious remodeling and decorating, made their house a thing of beauty, and Frederick, by self-denial, had turned his into a philanthropy, Mabel had elected to keep the agglomeration of stained glass and chocolate-colored clapboard she'd inherited just the way it was. The way it was was awful.

Mabel's long-departed grandparents had chosen wallpapers that wouldn't show the dirt. As the papers still hadn't been showing the dirt to any noticeable degree when her parents took over the house, the said parents had let them alone. Whether or not they were finally showing the dirt would have been difficult to ascertain. Whatever the pattern might once have been, it looked now like a great deal of undercooked pigs' liver.

By inheritance or pillage, Mabel had acquired a great deal of furniture. Unlike Emma, Mabel did not keep the overflow in her cellar. She preferred, as she often said, to enjoy her treasures. What enjoyment

Mabel derived from three hatstands with hangers made of real deer hooves, three worsted-worked love seats, and a large bronze statue of Atlas carrying an illuminated globe on his shoulders and having his private parts discreetly dealt with by means of a barometer set into his lower abdomen was a mystery not even Max Bittersohn would have cared to tackle. And that was just the foyer.

Sarah had to sit on one of the love seats for several minutes while Zeriah, the maid, a hard-bitten specimen from the wilds of upper New Hampshire who claimed she could lick her weight in wildcats and worked for Mabel, it was assumed, to keep in trim, went to find out if the mistress was in. This was routine procedure. If Sarah hadn't been on time to the dot, Mabel would have been out on the doorstep with blood in her eye.

In due course the lady of the house made her entrance. Mabel was a big woman like Aunt Appie, but a good deal dressier. Over the years she'd collected the wardrobes of several departed relatives, and naturally wanted to enjoy these treasures along with the rest. Today she had on a Voices of Spring number in green and yellow chiffon with trailing sleeves, trailing shoulder panels, and various other trailing bits here and there, all of them wildly aflutter as she tramped down the hall in her sensible brown oxfords. With her high color and masses of badly waved white hair, she looked something like a giant peony in a windstorm, Sarah thought. The peony, of course, would have been prettier.

"Well, Sarah, you finally made it," was her affectionate greeting. "I'm surprised you managed to spare the time."

Her bulbous blue eyes were fastened on Sarah's waistline as she spoke. "Nothing doing in the family line yet, eh? You don't have much luck with husbands, do you?"

"Oh, I shouldn't say that," Sarah replied with a wicked little smile she'd been practicing for just such a contingency. "You're looking well, Cousin Mabel. What an interesting dress you have on."

Mabel Kelling was not to be beguiled by flattery. She hated being told she looked well almost more than she hated being told she looked ill. She treated Sarah to an account of her latest brush with the Grim Reaper, a spectacular gastric upset designed, no doubt, to account for the meager fare of which they were about to partake and, with luck, to destroy her guest's appetite altogether.

Sarah didn't care, she hadn't come here to eat. She threaded her way among the hassocks and taborets to the morning room, accepted one of the many chairs there present, and waited patiently for Zeriah to come and serve her a grudging puddle of abominable sherry in one of Great-aunt Berengaria's ruby-glass goblets.

Mabel took the best of the chairs for herself, spent some time getting comfortable, then buckled down to business. "I suppose there are great doings over at Emma's this week. Everybody working for her full tilt so she can reap the glory as usual."

"It hasn't been all fun and games," Sarah was willing to concede in the interests of diplomacy. "I suppose you've heard about poor Charlie Daventer."

"Fell in the bathtub blind drunk and cracked his head open," Mabel replied with unconcealed relish. "I understand they found him stark naked except for a black-lace garter belt and a pair of rhinestone earrings."

"Cousin Mabel, whoever told you that? Isn't it amazing how vicious gossip gets around? Don't you often wonder who thinks up these wild yarns?"

"Oh, Sarah, don't try to pull that guileless act with me. Considering the scandals you've managed to get yourself mixed into, a person might think you'd know the facts of life by now. Everybody knows what Charlie Daventer was. Why do you think he never married? All that nonsense about being devoted to Emma. Huh!"

Mabel touched her sherry glass to her lips and brought it away with the puddle undiminished. "Is it true he's left his money to some young fellow he's been running around with?"

"Heavens, no. He's left it to the school for the handicapped. And I know that for a positive fact because Cousin Frederick's an executor and he told me so himself."

"Ah, I see. Then it was one of the male teachers from the school." Mabel treated herself to a genuine gulp of her sherry. "I can't say I'm surprised. I always did think there was something fishy about that place. All those do-gooders cooped up together with a pack of cripples. I must attend the next open house and see what's going on."

"Mabel, you wouldn't."

"Sarah, a woman in my position has a civic duty to keep an eye on the morals of the community. You wouldn't understand that, obviously. More sherry? Then let's go in to lunch," Mabel added without giving Sarah a chance to say yes or no.

"Frederick must be sick as a dog that Charlie didn't leave him anything," she observed as she tucked her flutters under her napkin. "Not that Fred needs it, surely. He's got the first dividend he ever collected, salted away in a Swiss bank to duck the income tax as Dolph must have told you."

"No, he never did. Dolph's fairly sound on the laws of slander."

"Slander? What's slander got to do with Charlie Daventer's money? You're getting more like your father every day of your life. I hope you can eat sardines."

Sarah thought she could, as there was only one of

them on her plate along with a paper-thin slice of tomato, half a gherkin, a wisp of lettuce, and a dab of mayonnaise. She said it looked delicious and changed the subject, not that she expected it to do much good. "Are you coming to the show tonight?"

"I haven't seen anybody offering me a ticket." Mabel snapped the tail off her sardine, large white dentures clicking sharply.

"You know Aunt Emma never gives anybody a complimentary ticket. If she did, she'd wind up papering the whole house and there'd be no money raised for charity."

"I thought charity began at home. What's it supposed to be in aid of this time? Dolph starting a home for retired barflies, now that he's collected all those empty beer bottles?"

"Oh, he doesn't have any. Ever since the bottle bill was passed, they've been making a fortune on the refunds." Sarah did enjoy watching Mabel wince. "The recycling center's wholly self-supporting now. They've added a lounge where they serve things to eat and have lots of comfortable chairs. Mary says one of the problems of being a street person is that you never get to sit down where it's really comfortable. Getting back to Aunt Emma, she's doing this one for the Visiting Nurses' Crutch and Wheelchair Fund. I just hope Ridpath Wale won't be needing their services tonight. He had a little fall at the dress rehearsal and twisted his ankle. You know Ridpath, don't you?"

Cousin Mabel gave her head the sort of toss Queen Elizabeth I might have used on Lord Burleigh. "I believe I may say so. He pestered me for years to marry him, as you apparently hadn't heard."

Sarah had not heard. She had been treated to similar confidences about other unlikely men. To do Mabel justice, some of them might have been almost halfway true. Mabel had, after all, been the only child of rich parents. As Dolph had once remarked, any girl could look beautiful sitting on top of a million dollars.

Mabel's fortune must be considerably bigger now than when she'd inherited it. It was beyond the realm of imagination that she'd ever touched a penny of her capital, or even dipped deeply into the accrued interest. Speculation on whom Mabel was going to leave her money to was a favorite rainy-day sport among the several branches of the Kelling clan.

"I've been wondering why Ridpath isn't married," she replied with calculated hypocrisy. "How romantic, Cousin Mabel. But why didn't you like him? Ridpath has such lovely manners, and he's quite good-looking, don't you think?"

"Looks aren't everything." Mabel was holding her gherkin by its stem and eating it in tiny nibbles, like an oversized chipmunk with an undersized nut. "I could never marry a man who gambles."

"Oh? No, I'm sure you couldn't. Does Ridpath gamble heavily?"

"The day I heard he was buying stock in some fly-by-night company that claimed to be making a camera that could develop its own film, I knew it could never be. I remember my sainted father telling me on my fourth birthday when he gave me my first very own safe-deposit key, 'You hang on to your municipal bonds, Mabel, and keep out of the stock market. It's no fit place for a respectable woman.' So Ridpath married somebody else, just to spite me."

"But he's not married now, is he?"

"No, she left him ages ago. They swept it all under the rug, of course, one of those nonsensical no-contest divorces citing irreconcilable differences. Huh! She couldn't reconcile herself to his throwing money down the drain, nor he to her carrying on with every man she could get her hooks into. Anyway, he drinks. Like a fish," Mabel added, waving the remains of her sardine around on her fork for emphasis.

"Does he?" said Sarah. "I hadn't noticed, particularly."

Mabel snorted. "You're hardly the most observant person in the world, are you? Otherwise, you might have observed who it is that new husband of yours takes with him on those so-called business trips he's always trotting off on."

"It's usually me. Anyway, I can hardly send a private detective to spy on him when he's one himself, can I?"

Sarah finished her sardine and ate the wilted lettuce, knowing she'd get a lecture on the starving people of Africa if she left anything but the pattern on her plate. "You mustn't fret about Max, Cousin Mabel. He'd never take another woman with him unless he could figure out a way to put her on his expense account, and he wouldn't do that anyway because it all comes out of his own pocket in the end. What about Jack Tippleton? He's something of a philanderer, I gather from the way he's been acting with one of the women in the cast, but Aunt Emma claims he's all talk and no action."

Mabel wasn't ready for Jack Tippleton, she hadn't finished with Ridpath Wale. "How did he sprain his ankle?"

"I don't think it's a sprain, just a wrench. He tripped over a piece of the scenery." That was stretching it a bit, but she certainly wasn't about to tell Mabel about those booby-trapped steps. "And no, he had not been drinking. There wasn't a drop of liquor anywhere."

"Don't be silly. Bottles hidden all over the set, no doubt, if only you'd had wits enough to see them. It does surprise me, I must say. Ridpath fancies himself such a great tennis player, one might have thought he'd be nimble enough not to go falling over his own feet. He plays all winter long at one of those indoor clubs to keep in trim, though don't ask me what for. Those places cost a fortune in dues, but what does he care? Easy come, easy go."

Mabel pushed out her chair and stood up. "I knew you wouldn't want dessert so I told Zeriah not to bother fixing any. You young women are all alike, fussing over your figures when you already look like walking skeletons. Next thing you know, you'll wind up with that anorexia nervosa which seems to be all the rage at the moment. Wasting away to a shadow. We'll have our tea in the morning room, Zeriah."

As Mabel led the way through her minefield of treasures, Sarah managed a glimpse at her own watch. She knew better than to trust any of Mabel's clocks, they were even less reliable than their owner's sources of information. One o'clock. Half an hour to go before succor arrived. She must try to think of this as an exercise in building character.

Mabel made a great deal of fuss over the tea tray. The tea wasn't worth the effort, but it did help to wash away the fishy taste of that lone sardine.

"Now," said Mabel when she'd got her own cup dosed with a drop of milk and five grains of sugar, "you asked me about Jack Tippleton. There's one man I've always felt really sorry for."

"You have?" Sarah almost dropped her teacup. "Why is that, Cousin Mabel?"

"Jack Tippleton was made the victim of one of the most cruel deceits I've ever heard of, and that's saying something, I can tell you. It happened back in the forties. Jack had gone into the Navy straight out of college. He'd been in the ROTC, so he got made some kind of junior lieutenant right away. I don't believe he ever saw combat duty or got a promotion, but that's beside the point. He was still in uniform when he came home and naturally he was the debs' delight. He had everything, you know—looks, money, and he danced the meanest tango in Pleasaunce."

Mabel gave herself more tea, absentmindedly ignoring Sarah's cup. "Well, this went on for quite a while. Jack went with this one and that one, but none of the girls managed to snare him. Then this little Martha Sorter blew into town, all fluffy ruffles and big brown eyes, visiting the Pences. That's Parker Pence's grandparents. Old Mrs. Pence and Martha's mother had been roommates at boarding school, or something. Anyway, the mother had died and the father was having a depression. Having a woman on the side, more likely, and didn't want his daughter underfoot. So to make a long story short, Ellen Pence sent for the girl and here she was."

Mabel drank some of her cooling tea. "Jack Tippleton fell for Martha in a big way. So did a few others, don't ask me why. Frederick made an awful ass of himself, as I recall, but of course no girl in her right mind was going to look at Fred if she could get Jack. Naturally the Tippletons checked out her background but they couldn't find a thing against her. Old Philadelphia family, father's business sound as a bell, daughter the only heiress, so they went ahead and gave their blessing.

"Sorter chartered a private train to take the Tippletons and the Pences to Philadelphia for the wedding, as I recall. Or maybe he simply sent them his private railway car. Anyway, it was quite a setout." Mabel sniffed to show what she thought of private railway cars. "So there they were, all moonlight and roses for the next few years with the newlyweds billing and cooing and the Tippletons going around patting themselves on the back about Jack's having made such a wonderful match. Then one fine day there's a piece in *The Wall Street Journal* hinting that Sorter's firm was heading for the rocks. Next

thing we knew, Sorter himself was splashed all over
the sidewalk in front of a New York hotel."

"Oh, no!" Sarah gasped.

Mabel Kelling nodded in agreeable recollection.
"They had to scrape him up with a shovel and bury
him in a bucket. In a pauper's grave, or he would
have been if his creditors could have found a way to
dig up the family plot and take that along with
everything else. So there's poor Jack, stuck with a
wife who hasn't a penny to her name. Can you imagine anything worse?"

"Yes, lots of things," Sarah told her. Being married
to Cousin Mabel, for instance, though she wasn't
reckless enough to say so. "I've been in a similar fix,
you know, and I came out of it all right."

"That remains to be seen. Besides, you had Walter's money, such as it was. Martha got nothing at
all except the undertaker's bill, which Cousin Beddoes insisted on paying when the Tippletons wouldn't
touch it. Don't ask me why he did, though it always
seemed to me that second son of Martha's favors Bed
a little around the eyes. You needn't repeat that to
Emma."

"I shouldn't dream of it," Sarah assured her. "Then
Jenicot has older brothers. I hadn't realized."

"Oh yes, three of them. If it weren't for those boys,
I daresay Jack would have found some way to get
out of the marriage once he realized what a terrible
mistake he'd made, but he could hardly take the
chance with no other grandsons in the family and
his father so keen on keeping up the name. There's
nothing shaky about the Tippleton money, you know.
I'm not saying Jack's any great intellect, but you've
got to give him credit for knowing which side his
bread's buttered on. His parents hadn't any come-
back about the marriage because it was Jack's mother
who checked out Martha's connections and her father
who ran the Dun & Bradstreet on Sorter's finances.

They were decent enough to Martha afterward, all things considered, but naturally they could never feel the same toward her again."

Mabel waved the teapot vaguely in Sarah's direction and set it down again. "Of course Jack didn't, either. He'd been stepping around a little ever since her first pregnancy, but he'd been discreet about it up till then. Once the bloom was off the rose, he went ahead and did as he pleased, though he's managed to stay out of any real scrape as far as I know."

"And you would know," Sarah murmured.

Mabel accepted the compliment with a smirk. "I'm a pretty hard person to fool. But anyway, that's how it's gone ever since. Martha tried every trick in the book to hang on to Jack, but she didn't get far. She'd been one of those early bloomers who lose their looks once they start having children."

"I think she's perfectly beautiful still."

"Humph. What good's your opinion going to do her? For heaven's sake, Sarah, don't go turning yourself into another sunshine girl like Appie. One in the family's already more than the rest of us can stomach."

Mabel emitted an all-purpose snort of derision for the world's follies. "Sweetness and light didn't help Martha any. She even went ahead and had that last child when she was old enough to know better. I suppose she thought a cute little daughter would keep Jack home nights. It might have worked, if Jenicot had been somebody else's cute little daughter. I told Martha time and time again that she might as well quit trying because it wasn't going to pan out no matter what she did, but I should have saved my breath. Try to be nice to a person, and what thanks do you get?"

"These things are sent to test us, Cousin Mabel." Sarah looked at her watch again, making no bones about it this time. "Tell me about Sebastian Frostedd. Is he as black as he's painted?"

No, it appeared he was a great deal worse. Mabel wasn't half done mincing Sebastian to shreds when Heatherstone was at the door with a totally superfluous rug over his arm to usher Sarah to the car. On a final volley of acrimony, she ended her visit.

Chapter 15

"Enjoy your lunch, Sarah?"

"About as much as I expected to."

Sarah settled back against the gray velvet upholstery and smiled at Heatherstone's gray broadcloth back as he steered the aging limousine homeward at a sedate thirty miles an hour. He seldom bothered to change into his livery; he'd worn his usual black box jacket to the crematorium. No doubt he'd put on the braided jacket and cap on purpose to give Cousin Mabel something else to steam about. The Heatherstones must manage to extract a good deal of fun from their job, one way and another. Maybe Zeriah did, too, though Sarah couldn't see how.

"What's my aunt up to now?" she asked.

"She went off by herself in the doodlebug. She wanted to check things out for tonight at the auditorium, and pick up some flowers for tomorrow at the florist's. She doesn't want to take any more out of the garden. It's already looking kind of thin."

"Why couldn't she bring back the baskets after the show?"

"Oh, she'll be sending those to the nursing home or somewhere. You know Mrs. Kelling. I suppose we might have brought 'em back tonight if we were having the cast party. Too bad we had to call it off, but it couldn't be helped. Anyway, I expect most of them will be coming tomorrow. She said something about you arranging the flowers when she gets back, if you wouldn't mind."

"Not at all, I'd love to. Is there anything else she'd like me to do in the meantime?"

"She didn't mention anything to me. You might as well take a little rest for yourself. You won't get much tonight or tomorrow. We've already got about a hundred people coming for the memorial gathering, and I expect she'll invite a few dozen more before the day's out."

"How in the world do you all three keep it up?" Sarah marveled.

"Oh, we're used to it, and we wouldn't have it any other way. Never a dull moment, that's for sure. Our son's been after us to retire and move in with him, but we tell him we're perfectly happy with Mrs. Kelling and don't want to quit till she kicks us out."

"You know she'd never do that. I hope you'll be together for a long time yet."

This was getting sentimental. He'd be embarrassed. Sarah changed the subject.

"Heatherstone, have you been down cellar in the past couple of days?"

"Just to get wine for the table. Why do you ask?"

"I've been thinking about Ernestina. She'd have been so awkward to take away, I'm wondering if whoever stole her might simply have hidden her someplace right in the house. Then when they'd collected the ransom money, assuming they ever get around to telling us how to pay it, they'd only have to say, 'Go look behind the furnace,' or wherever."

"She's not behind the furnace, I can tell you that. But you know, Sarah, that's not such a dumb idea. There's certain things Mrs. Kelling doesn't expect Mrs. Heatherstone and me to do, and keeping track of that cellar is one of them. We generally get some college kid in once or twice a year to clean it up and straighten things out. Unless one of the family came along and started rooting around, you know how they do, I suppose you could slide the painting in underneath something else and it wouldn't be noticed for months. I tell you what I'd do, though. I'd put Ernestina in the attic. It's nice and dry up there and she wouldn't be so apt to mildew."

"That's a thought. I'll go up and have a look when we get back. I'm sure you and Mrs. Heatherstone are far too busy getting ready for tomorrow."

"Well, you know how it is. Mrs. Heatherstone's going to be baking all afternoon, which leaves me to do the silver and the rest of it. Added to which, Mrs. Kelling's invited Mr. Frederick and the Tippletons to supper before the show and we're trying to get everything organized so we can scoot off right after dessert. Got to be early if you want a seat down front."

"That's right, there aren't any reserved seats, are there?"

"Nope, not a one. Mrs. Kelling knows her own friends would buy them up first crack off the bat, and that wouldn't be fair to the rest. First come, first served is the way it's always been and always will be as long as she's running the show. Which still leaves Mrs. Heatherstone and me as free as anybody else to get down there early and grab ourselves a good spot, is how we look at it."

"And you couldn't be more right," Sarah agreed. "I'm just praying everything goes without a hitch tonight. I don't mind telling you I'll be relieved to see Aunt Emma taking her curtain calls safe and sound."

Even though these would be her last ones. No matter, Emma Kelling would find a new cause to hurl herself into. Provided she got the chance.

Sarah stayed in the car until Heatherstone had driven it into the carriage shed. She couldn't see any good place to hide Ernestina here. The space was too open, and the cars were always coming and going. There'd be too many chances for the painting to be noticed, however well it was disguised.

She didn't think much of Heatherstone's suggestion about the attic, either, though she wouldn't have hurt his feelings by saying so. Humping that heavy stretcher with its precious, fragile covering up two long flights of stairs, past two bedrooms whose occupants might or might not have succumbed to the drugged Slepe-o-tite, would have taken more nerve than brains. Any member of the cast must know Emma often went up there hunting for props. How could they be sure she wouldn't develop a sudden yen for a feather boa to set off her bustle, and stumble over Ernestina in the course of the hunt?

Nevertheless, as soon as she'd changed out of her good linen suit, Sarah went up and had a look around. As expected, she found nothing that hadn't been there a week ago except a family of newly hatched spiders whose acquaintance she didn't much care to cultivate. Now her duty to Heatherstone was done. On to the cellar.

The cellar, she was forced to admit after over an hour's futile tugging and pushing and crawling over the discards of the decades, was a bust. What next? Food, she decided. Cousin Mabel's sardine hadn't stayed with her long. She went upstairs, cleaned off the dust and cobwebs at the flower-room sink, and stepped into the kitchen.

"Hello, Mrs. Heatherstone. Would I be in your way if I made myself a sandwich?"

"After that big lunch at Miss Mabel's?" Mrs. Heatherstone smiled as she slid a tray of patty shells into the oven. "How about a slice of the roast lamb we had last night? It might go good with a little chutney. Or I could heat you a bowl of soup."

"Lamb will be fine, thanks. Please go on with what

you're doing. I understand my aunt got carried away with the guest list."

"She generally does, but I don't mind. It sort of makes up for us not having the cast party. What did Her Majesty give you to eat, may I ask?"

"A sardine."

"A whole one, all to yourself? Getting reckless in her old age, isn't she? I suppose Miss Mabel was pretty cut up about Mr. Daventer."

Sarah shook her head. "If she was, she didn't show it. As a matter of fact, she was downright bitchy."

"That's a switch. Any time I ever saw them together, she was all over him like poison ivy on a stone wall. Want a cup of tea to wet your whistle? The kettle's just on the boil."

"If you'll have one with me." Sarah knew her old friend ran on frequent cups of tea, the way a racing car has to keep getting refilled with gasoline.

Mrs. Heatherstone filled two of the old Dedham Potteries mugs, decorated with bands of white rabbits on a blue ground, handed one to Sarah, and sat down with the other at the end of the kitchen table, slewing her chair around so she could keep an eye on the oven.

"Have to watch those patty shells like a hawk," she remarked. "My land, it's nice having you here, Sarah. Just like old times. Remember how you wouldn't drink your milk unless I gave it to you in one of these bunny mugs, as you called them?"

Sarah laughed. "Wouldn't I? I'd never have got away with that at home. You spoiled me rotten out here, and how I loved it. I do remember crying when Father came to get me. He was none too happy about that, as I recall."

"I don't suppose he was happy about much of anything just then." Mrs. Heatherstone took a dainty sip of her tea. "You haven't had the most cheerful life in the world yourself, have you, Sarah? But you're all right now?"

"Oh yes. Being married to Max is—I can't tell you what a difference it's made."

"Too bad he has to be away so much."

"Cousin Mabel said something to that effect, only in a different tone of voice. But I get to go with him quite often, you know, and that's glorious fun. I never traveled before. And when he has to go by himself, he brings me lovely presents. Horrid thing to say, isn't it? But you know my parents never went in for such frivolities, and neither did Alexander. He used to buy me Milky Ways sometimes."

Sarah fell silent, thinking about the last time Alexander had bought her Milky Ways. Mrs. Heatherstone leaned across the table and patted her hand.

"There, there, dearie. Alexander was a fine man and I know you were the apple of his eye, but being married to your father's best friend was no life for a pretty young thing like you. I still say it happened for the best, and so does Mr. Heatherstone. How about a cookie?"

"I'd love one. I'll take it with me and let you get on with your work. Don't fret, I was well taught not to strew crumbs around the floor."

Sarah gave Mrs. Heatherstone a light kiss on the cheek and went out. So many memories. Those of the times she'd spent in this house had been among the happiest, until last summer. Maybe she'd drop into the dining room and say hello to the lions for auld lang syne.

Oh, for heaven's sake! How blind could a person be? Sarah blinked, and started to run. Seconds later, crouched under the dining-room table, she was gazing up at forty-eight square feet of dirty old canvas.

She couldn't see Ernestina, but Ernestina was there, hidden by the table's deep apron, her wide stretcher propped up on top of the massive brass crank handles that had to be turned to open the top and insert the extension leaves. It was so simple, so obvious. It was ridiculous. Sarah began to laugh.

Heatherstone heard her, all the way from the butler's pantry. He came in, still clutching his silver-polishing chamois.

"What's so funny, Sarah? Whatever are you doing under that table?"

"Saying hello to Ernestina. Scrooch down and have a look."

Carefully inching his trouser legs up over his knees, the elderly manservant obeyed. "Well, I'll be darned! Can you beat that? I'd never have thought of looking there in a million years."

"I should have thought of it sooner, considering how many times I've parked Uncle Bed's detective stories under here so Aunt Emma wouldn't see what I was reading. Mrs. Heatherstone and I got to reminiscing, and it must have jogged my brain. Come on, let's tell her. She can't leave her patty shells."

"She'll leave them for this. Wait, now, don't try to get Ernestina down by yourself. Elsie! Elsie, come here, quick."

This was the first time in her life Sarah had heard either of the Heatherstones use the other's first name in the presence of a Kelling. She laughed again, though softly, because she wouldn't have hurt their feelings for the world.

"What's the matter, George?" His wife hurried in, bringing no trace of the patty shells with her. She'd even whisked off her apron, though she'd forgotten to put it down. "Are you all right?"

"I'm fine. Sarah's found Ernestina."

"Where? Show me, so I can believe it."

"Right under here," Sarah called from her lowly roost. "Up against the bottom of the table."

"Well, did you ever?" Mrs. Heatherstone squatted and peered. "If that doesn't beat all! And to think I dusted this table myself, only this morning. Whatever possessed you to think of looking there, Sarah?"

"You and the bunny mugs, I suppose. Do you think you two could steady the stretcher while I ease her off these handles? I don't want her to come crashing down on my head, and wind up wearing her for a collar."

"All right, we've got her. Just take it slow and easy."

They must look awfully silly, Sarah thought, the three of them hunkered down underneath that enormous table like three toads under a mushroom, but they managed together to free Ernestina and lower her gently to the carpet.

"Must have taken a flock of monkeys to put her up there," Heatherstone grunted as he straightened up and dusted off his trousers. "Let's have a look at her. She didn't get scratched?"

Newspapers had been carefully laid over the face of the painting to protect the surface. Wednesday's Pleasaunce *Pathfinder*, Sarah noticed. It must have been lying around the living room the night Ernestina was taken down. She gathered up the sheets and laid them aside.

"Not a scratch as far as I can see. They took good care of her, at any rate. Do you suppose the three of us could get her back into her frame?"

"If you don't mind, Sarah, I don't think we'd better try," Mrs. Heatherstone objected. "Mr. Heatherstone's not supposed to do any heavy lifting these days on account of his blood pressure, though he won't thank me for telling you. I vote we leave Ernestina right where she is till we can get somebody in who knows how to handle her. Nobody's going to step on her under the table, and we can always say we put her there ourselves, which is true enough as far as it goes, if anybody happens to notice."

"You're right," Sarah admitted. "I just thought it

would be a nice surprise for Aunt Emma to come home and find her hanging back where she belongs."

"If you ask me, Mrs. Kelling's had about all the surprises she needs for a while. Besides, she likes that one you did of her better. So do I. Now if you'll excuse me, I've got to get back to my patty shells."

"And I to the silver," said Heatherstone. "Oh, there goes that darned phone again. Answer it like good girl, will you, Sarah? It'll be somebody for Mrs. Kelling."

It was, but the caller was quite willing to unburden herself to Sarah.

"This is Marcia Pence. Parker's mother, you know. I'm sorry to bother you with such a tiny problem when you must be up to your ears about tonight and tomorrow. The thing of it is, my mother's living with us now. She's not too well, and can't get around much. She sent a little token to Mrs. Heatherstone a few days ago—they've always been special pals for one reason and another, and she hasn't been able to get over there because of her infirmity. Mother was rather expecting Mrs. Heatherstone would give her a ring or drop a note. You know how old people are, little things become so important. Anyway, since she hasn't heard, she's dreadfully upset for fear Mrs. Heatherstone didn't get her present. I'm sure it's just that Mrs. Heatherstone's been too busy to bother, with the show and everything."

"No, she'd have taken time to acknowledge a gift, no matter how busy she was. Could it have been held up at the post office, I wonder?"

"It wasn't mailed. I'd meant to run Mother over in the car so she could deliver it in person, but she'd been having one of her bad days and Jenicot Tippleton happened to be here with Parker. She mentioned to Mother that she and Parker were on their way to Emma's for a rehearsal, so Mother asked them to take her package along. It was just a box of candy, actually."

That rang a bell. "Not liqueur cherries, by any chance?"

"Why, yes, as a matter of fact. That was a little standing joke between Mother and Mrs. Heatherstone, that they both adore liqueur cherries. Mother had her birthday last weekend and she got no fewer than four boxes of them, so she thought she'd like to share her loot. Then Jenny did remember to take them?"

Sarah hedged. "I'm afraid what happened was that Mrs. Heatherstone got her cherries all right, but didn't realize they were from your mother. I believe they were handed to her just about the same time as Aunt Emma was telling her there'd be extra guests for dinner, and things got a bit confused. I'll explain the situation to her right now, shall I?"

Marcia Pence said that would be wonderful and that she'd be seeing Sarah at the performance but didn't suppose they'd have much of a chance to chat, especially since she'd have a flute to her mouth. She moaned a bit about not being able to have the usual cast party after the show but quite understood how Emma felt and promised they'd be over tomorrow afternoon unless Mother took a turn for the worse. Sarah said something polite and hung up, much puzzled.

Whatever had possessed Jenicot and Parker to hand the cherries over for Sebastian Frostedd to bring? He'd got here before the young hero and heroine, she recalled, but not all that long before. Maybe they'd planned to stop for some errand on the way and hadn't known how long it would take, but what difference would it have made whether Mrs. Heatherstone got her present right away or a little later?

But what a mingy, contemptible trick for Sebastian Frostedd to pull on Mrs. Heatherstone, taking credit for her sick old friend's gift. Max would call him a lousy bastard, Sarah thought, and Max would be hitting the nail smack on the head. She went out to the kitchen and delivered Marcia Pence's message, trying not to let her own opinion of the episode color her speech.

Mrs. Heatherstone took a different view. "Imagine that. Mr. Frostedd must have thought I was making an awful fuss over him just for doing a little favor. I suppose he didn't want to embarrass me by pointing out my mistake. Dear old Mrs. Sabine, wasn't it sweet of her to think of me? I'll whip up a few fruit tarts and get Mr. Heatherstone to swing by on our way to the show so we can drop them off. Mrs. Sabine always loved my fruit tarts."

So that little matter was taken care of, and Sarah had further proof that Sebastian Frostedd was the rotten apple everybody claimed he was. She wondered even more now whether Sebastian had paid a late call on Charles Daventer. He could easily have thought up an excuse to stop by and wangle a nightcap; he'd know Emma wouldn't keep her old friend up late. Maybe he'd even helped Charlie into his pajamas before clubbing him over the head and staging the accident.

But that would mean Sebastian's having faked Frederick's prize evidence, too, and why ever would he have done that? Did he have that crazy a sense of humor? And would he have hung around the scene of a murder he'd just committed long enough to provide so copious a clue?

On the other hand, he could have stayed drinking with Charlie long enough to make sure the man was thoroughly fuddled, borrowed Charlie's door key, then sneak back later and kill him in his sleep. But why

kill him at all? Why should he or anybody want
Charles Daventer dead?

Why keep asking herself stupid questions? Why
didn't she sit down calmly and reasonably, and try
to sort out the facts?

Chapter 16

All right, then, what did she know? Little enough. She knew Ernestina had never left the house. She knew there were at least two people involved in the abduction. No, she didn't know that but she thought it was a safe assumption. Balancing the huge painting on those four brass crank handles without ruffling up the smooth layer of loose newspapers that had been laid over the surface would be tricky enough for a team, and surely impossible for a person working alone.

She further surmised at least one of the thieves must be well acquainted with her aunt. Otherwise how could they have known the dining-room table had an apron deep enough to hide the painting, and cranks underneath that could be used to hold it out of sight? Granted, guests didn't go crawling under their hostess's dining tables as a rule, but one might always drop a napkin or something, happen to notice the hardware while picking it up, and file away the information in one of those odd mental corners from which things pop out when they're wanted. And there were the jugs of Slepe-o-tite too. Yes, that could count as a known.

She knew also that five separate ransom notes—Sarah supposed they might as well be called ransom notes—had been delivered in various melodramatic ways, that none of them had given any usable information except the one that mentioned a ridiculously small ransom with no instructions about paying it. All that cloak-and-dagger correspondence to so little purpose was perhaps the oddest part of this whole affair. It looked as if the extortionists were more interested in boiling the pot than in skimming off the cash. Was Ernestina only a means to some other end? A harassment campaign against Emma Kelling? A plot to drive her out of her house? What made them think she'd ever knuckle under?

More questions, fewer answers. And here came Aunt Emma with her bundles. Sarah gave it up and went to fetch in the flowers.

"We have a surprise for you, Aunt Emma."

"A happy one, I hope. If not, don't tell me. What is it?"

"It's Ernestina. We've found her."

"Where?"

"Under the dining-room table."

"Impossible! How would she get there?"

Sarah gave what explanation she could. Emma Kelling shook her head. "Utterly ridiculous! How did they know I mightn't decide to give a small formal dinner party, and want the leaves taken out?"

"Don't ask me, but there she was."

"Well, I must say this strikes me as a singularly ill-run operation."

Emma's hand strayed to the gold pencil dangling on her bosom. Sarah had a wild thought that she was about to go get one of her blue notebooks and take charge.

"We left Ernestina under the table, lying on the rug," she told her aunt. "She was too heavy for the Heatherstones and me to put back into the frame."

"Heavens, yes. You mustn't dream of trying. Anyway, now that she's down, I may as well go ahead and have her cleaned. Do let's remember to lock the dining-room door tomorrow, though, in case somebody happens to bring a child along. That dining-room table always draws them like a magnet, I can't think why. As a rule, of course, I let them play there all they like. There's really nothing fragile within grabbing distance, and it keeps them out from under foot. I do hope to goodness nobody does bring a child. I don't know about you, but I'm beginning to feel a trifle frayed about the edges. Now about those flowers, Sarah. The best thing would be to leave them conditioning in the plant room overnight and do them in the morning, if you think you can manage."

"No problem. I shan't have anything much else to do. Or will I?"

"I can't think what, though no doubt something will come to me. Take them into the flower room, then. We did leave the buckets there, didn't we?"

"I'll go see."

Sarah gathered up the bright sheaves, sniffing at the freesias as she went. Aunt Emma was always careful to choose cut flowers for their fragrance as well as their beauty, unlike Aunt Appie, who'd presented Sarah and Max with a basketful of Christmas greens that smelled like a courting tomcat once they were brought into a warm room.

"Don't forget we're having early supper tonight," her aunt called after her. "If you're planning to change, you'd better do it soon."

That might be taken as a hint. Sarah quickly stripped the flowers of excess foliage, cut the stems at a slant, and plunged them into water. Then she went upstairs and put on a loose cotton gauze shift with some silver, agate, and turquoise jewelry Max had bought her off the sidewalk in Santa Fe. The costume was quite elegant enough for Emma Kelling's table, or anybody else's she was likely to get invited to, yet it would be practical for backstage. She was looking forward to doing the makeups again tonight.

By the time she'd fixed her hair and got back

downstairs, Cousin Frederick and all three Tippletons had arrived. Jack was working his charm on
Emma in an offhand way, and devoting more serious
attention to his drink. Frederick was concentrating
wholeheartedly on Martha. For a noncharmer, he
appeared to be managing well enough. Martha looked
more alive than Sarah had ever seen her before. The
color in her face hadn't been artificially induced, she
was smiling at something Frederick was telling her.
Those enormous dark eyes were, if not actually dancing, at least giving the impression that they wouldn't
mind trying.

Jenicot was sitting by herself on one of Emma's
brocaded satin love seats, staring at her mother as
if Martha were some odd specimen that had got out
of its bottle. Sarah went over and sat down beside
her.

"All set for tonight, Jenicot?"

"I guess so. If I don't forget my lines."

"Why should you? You were fine at rehearsal last
night. Oh, by the way, Mrs. Heatherstone got her
candy."

"Candy?" Jenicot's eyes went as big as her mother's. "What candy?"

"That box of liqueur cherries Mrs. Pence's mother
asked you and Parker to bring over. Mrs. Heatherstone hadn't thanked Mrs. Sabine because somehow
or other it got to be Sebastian Frostedd who handed
them to her, and she thought they were from him."

"Oh, that. I'd forgotten. It was so totally unimportant. Shouldn't we be eating, so we can get to the
theater on time?"

"Don't fret, I'm sure Aunt Emma has us timed to
the second."

That was not what Sarah wanted to say. Little
witch! The candy had not been totally unimportant
to the person who sent it, or to the one Mrs. Sabine

had wanted to have it. Jenicot Tippleton needed her ears pinned back.

Sarah did not intend to do the pinning, though, not tonight. She wasn't about to turn anybody's first-night jitters into a full-scale fit. She made another noncommittal remark or two, to which Jenicot responded in surly monosyllables. Then Cousin Frederick said something, and Martha Tippleton laughed out loud. It was a sound Sarah hadn't thought she could make.

"Your mother's in great spirits tonight," she said to Jenicot. "I've never seen her looking so well."

"She's the most beautiful woman who ever lived." The ferocity in Jenicot's voice was startling. So the girl did have some feelings, after all. "Don't you think so? Honestly, Sarah?"

That was a plea Sarah could never have refused even if she'd wanted to. "I think she's absolutely ravishing," she replied with perfect truth. "I was saying so to one of my cousins at lunchtime, as a matter of fact."

"Which one?"

"Mabel."

"Oh, her." Jenicot went back to scowling at the hearthrug. After a while, she got around to speaking again. "The thing of it is, Mama's—well, she wasn't exactly a kid when I was born. My brother Marsden's almost forty, you know."

"Actually I didn't. It hardly seems possible your mother could have a son that age."

This was what Jenicot wanted to hear, but it wasn't enough. "Your Cousin Mabel thinks Mama's a mess. She told Mama so."

Sarah laughed. "Heavens, you don't care about that, do you? Mabel thinks everybody's a mess. Have a cheese straw."

"I know, but—" Jenicot nibbled the end off her

cheese straw. "What if—you know—other people—"

Whatever Jenicot was about to confide, Sarah
never got to hear. The doorbell's wild jangling startled them all into silence, then Gillian Bruges flung
herself into the room.

"Mrs. Kelling! Mrs. Kelling!"

She was screaming and sobbing, stumbling over
the carpet. Heatherstone was at her heels, making
agitated noises. A youngish man in a red T-shirt and
some kind of uniform cap was beside him, talking
fast and loud, making oversized gestures. Sarah
barely had time to gasp at what a wreck Gillian
looked when the uninvited arrival was hurling herself into Mrs. Kelling's arms, burying her face on
Mrs. Kelling's shoulder.

Emma was trying to support her, fend her off, and
get her to make sense, and not having much luck all
around. "Gillian, what's the matter? What happened? Were you in an accident?"

"She got mugged."

This was the strange man speaking. He'd remembered his cap, and snatched it off. "I picked her up
at the corner of Main and Temple. I'm a cabbie, in
case you're wondering. I was on my way back to the
garage and I see this woman standing out in the
road waving me down. She looks like she's been hit
by a truck. So I stop and ask her what's the matter?
She tells me these two guys forced her off the road,
dragged her out of her car, beat her up, and took off
in the car. She was pretty hysterical, like she is now.
I said I better take her to the police station but she
kept yelling, 'No! No! Mrs. Kelling.' So naturally I
figured she must mean you. I hope it's okay."

"Oh yes, quite all right." There was a sigh in Emma's voice. "Hush, Gillian, you're safe now. Get her
some brandy, Heatherstone. Oh, and pay this kind
man his fare."

"Hey, that's okay. I don't want any money. I wouldn't feel right."

The man was backing toward the door, clutching his cap in front of him with both hands. "Just so I know she's okay. You better get some ice on that eye, miss."

In a confusion of thank yous and how dreadfuls, he was gone before Heatherstone, who'd been trying to get Gillian to sip some brandy, could see him to the door. After a few swallows of the brandy, Gillian calmed down enough to show her face. It was a mess. She must have been knocked down and had her head rubbed in the dirt. An ugly scrape disfigured her left cheek. The eye was red and puffed, swelling for a shiner. She was filthy, trembling, still half distraught.

"He should have taken her to the police station," Cousin Frederick was insisting.

"Or the hospital," Martha said. "Shall I call an ambulance?"

That set Gillian off again. "No, please! Let me stay here. I'll be all right. Truly, Mrs. Kelling."

"But we must report the theft of your car."

"The cabbie did. He stopped a cruiser. They know already. They asked me questions. I showed them my registration."

"Where was it?" Sarah asked her.

Gillian only stared.

"If they robbed you and took your car," Sarah repeated slowly, "how did you still have your registration? Where was it?"

"In my purse. They didn't take that. See?"

She showed them a little oblong of purple leather, still dangling from her shoulder by the narrowest possible strap. There was nothing much inside but a lipstick, comb, door key, and a slim card case.

"Did they take your money?"

"I didn't have much. Just a ten-dollar bill. Maybe

that's why they hit me so hard. I—" Before anybody could grab her, Gillian slid to the floor.

Jack Tippleton wasn't being very gallant by his damsel in distress, Sarah noted. It was Heatherstone and Cousin Frederick who got Gillian up on the sofa and Jenicot who ran for ice to put on her face. The eye was almost shut now, turning purple.

"She'll never be able to go on," said Martha, taking the ice bag from her daughter and laying it against Gillian's face.

"But I've got to!" Gillian pushed the ice away, sat up, and flopped back. "Only my head hurts so."

"I hope she doesn't have a concussion," Emma fretted. "Heatherstone, you'd better call an ambulance."

"No, don't," Gillian pleaded. "I'll be all right if you'll just let me rest here."

"But, Gillian, we can't all go off and leave you alone." Jack Tippleton had finally found his voice.

"I'll stay with her," Sarah volunteered.

"You can't," said Emma Kelling. "You'll have to sing Constance."

"Me? Aunt Emma, you can't mean it."

"Certainly I mean it. You managed nicely the other night with poor Charlie. Sarah, there is nobody else available, it's two hours to curtain time, and I do not propose to argue the matter. Now come along to supper, everybody. Gillian, do you think you could eat something?"

"I'm afraid I'd be sick. I just want to be quiet."

"Best thing for her," said Frederick. "Come on, Emma, let's put on the feed bag. Hurry up, Sarah. A full belly maketh a stiff upper lip."

Chapter 17

The meal Mrs. Heatherstone set out in the breakfast room was a simple one: mainly chowder, fruit, and cheese. Even that was too much for Sarah. She nibbled a pilot biscuit and took a spoonful or two of the chowder, but there was a lump in the middle of her chest the food couldn't seem to get past. After a few tries, she gave up.

"Aunt Emma, may I be excused? If I've got to do Constance, I'd better take a look at my lines."

"Of course, dear. Don't be too long about it, though. We'll have to leave in fifteen minutes if we're to have time to change. And, oh dear, I'm afraid you'll still have to help with the makeups."

Frederick, who'd dispatched his chowder with the speed of an old bachelor used to catch-as-catch-can dining, shoved back his chair. "I'll come with you, Sarah."

"But don't you want anything more to eat?" Emma asked him.

"No. Fruit makes me bilious and cheese is too binding. Come on, Sarah. Let's run through that number where you tell me you love me madly."

"All right, but we mustn't disturb Gillian. Come into the dining room and shut the door."

Once they were alone, though, Sarah didn't begin to sing. Instead, she beckoned him over to where Lady Ernestina and her dove lay staring up at the

175

underside of the table. "Let's put her back the way she was," she whispered.

"What for?" Frederick hissed back.

"I want to see whether we can manage it by ourselves."

"Oh, I get you. Detecting. Good show."

The two of them crawled under the table and went to work. It was surprisingly easy once they got the hang of taking one end at a time. All they had to do was raise the top of the stretcher and hook it over the handles at one end of the table, then boost the bottom and slide it into place over the other pair of handles, so in fact they never had to juggle the full weight of the painting. They had Ernestina back inside the apron in about two minutes, singing loudly all the while for the benefit of those in the breakfast room.

Then Frederick held the book for Sarah while she tried out her lines for the opener. Then they heard, "Come along, you two, we've no more time to waste."

That was Emma, herding her flock together. "Now let's see. I have the list of numbers for Gillian, and that cordless telephone Little Bed gave me for my birthday. Oh, and the aspirin and the ice bucket. For her face, you know. Poor girl, what a dreadful thing to happen just now. Sarah, you can't possibly think this has anything to do with—you know what. Can you? I'm actually having a small qualm about whether I ought to cancel the performance," she murmured, so softly that nobody but Sarah and Frederick could hear.

"You mustn't do that," Sarah told her. "We've already had our calamity for tonight, I think. I doubt very much that anything will go wrong at the theater."

"I certainly hope you're right."

"She'd better be," said Frederick. "I've personally hired two of Sergeant Formsby's men to stand guard backstage all through the performance. If they slip up, they'll have to whistle for their pay and I've told 'em so."

"Fred, you did that for me? My dear, I'm touched."

"Now, Emma, don't start slobbering over me. I did it for myself as much as anybody. I'm in this circus, too, you know. Go check your patient, and let's get started."

They went into the drawing room, where Gillian Bruges was still lying inert under a mohair throw on one of the sofas. "Gillian, are you awake?"

"Unh? Oh." The eye that was still operable opened. "Yes, Mrs. Kelling."

"My dear, we have to leave now. I'm putting a telephone and the numbers for the police and the hospital right here on this table beside you. And here's some aspirin and a carafe of water, and more ice for your face if you need it. You know where the bathroom is, don't you?"

"Yes, I can manage. Thank you, Mrs. Kelling."

"Now we'll make sure all the doors and windows are locked and the burglar alarms switched on so you'll be perfectly safe. I wish there were a neighbor I could get to come in and sit with you, but I'm afraid they're all coming to the show."

"It doesn't matter. I'm used to being alone in my apartment."

"Then you just get some rest and we'll see you later."

"Good luck with the show. I'm sorry I let you down."

Emma straightened the mohair throw as a last proprietary gesture and went out, counting noses.

"Let's see. Three, five, six of us plus the two Heatherstones. Too many for the Buick. You people did walk over, didn't you, Martha?"

"Yes, we thought it would make one fewer car in the parking lot. Jenny will be coming home with

Parker, I expect. She can sit in her father's lap on the way over."

"Oh, let her ride with me," said Sarah. "Max told me he'd try to make it back for the performance. If by any wild chance he does, we'll need another car anyway."

This was wishful thinking, but Sarah didn't feel like being squashed in with Jack Tippleton. She needed time to brood.

She didn't get it, of course. The too-often-silent Jenicot chattered nervously all the way to the auditorium, mostly along the lines of, "Aren't you scared to death, having to jump in at the last minute without even a proper rehearsal?" which didn't do much for Sarah's faltering morale. Jenicot herself was plainly in a state of near panic, though she tried to cover up with far too much semihysterical laughter. Much as she disrelished what lay ahead of her, Sarah was glad when the short ride was over.

At least her demure village maiden's costume was no great chore to get into. Sarah put on the polka-dot dress, tied the apron over it, found to her relief that the corkscrew curls and the flirty cap were all of a piece and pulled them over her own hair. Then she painted her face with china-doll spots of rouge on the cheeks, and went to cope with Aunt Emma's bustle.

She found she wasn't needed. Martha Tippleton was already in Emma's dressing room, and the two of them were having a lovely time. "Remember when I first came to Pleasaunce and you got me into your little theater group?" Martha was saying. "I played Lady Windermere and you were my wicked mother. We thought we were being so terribly racy. Turn around so I can get at those hooks. Did you know you've got writing on your bustle?"

"Oh yes, some nonsense the boys got into ages ago," Emma lied with an ease that astonished her niece. "Where's that mermaid's tail thing that goes over it, Sarah?"

"Right here. Want me to put it on?"

"No, we'll manage. Run along and get started on the makeups. You do know your lines?"

"I think so. If I dry up, you'll have to bail me out, Mrs. Tippleton."

"Please say Martha. I'm not really your mother, you know. I'm sure you'll be fine, Sarah. It's hardly the thing to say under the circumstances, but I never did feel altogether at ease with Gillian. She's an odd sort of girl, don't you think? Aside from her predilection for my too-frequently loving husband, that is."

Martha flushed. "That was in atrocious taste. I don't know what's got into me tonight."

"Something you could have used any time these past thirty years, in my candid opinion," Emma rejoined. "I do wish we hadn't had to leave Gillian alone in the house. Like her or not, she's my responsibility."

"You can phone her during the intermission."

"But she might be asleep. I'd hate to wake her up just to relieve my own conscience."

"You'll think of something," Martha said. "You always do. There, your fishtail's on straight. Now struggle into this."

Martha hopped up on a chair, dragging the billows of purple taffeta with her. Sarah saw there was nothing here for her to do, and went out to the makeup table, trying to remember her lines for the opening scene. She had rather a lot to do then, between her ballad of unrequited love and her dialogue with her stage mother. Fortunately, Martha would have far more lines than she, but Sarah didn't want to have to get by on sobs and flutters alone.

After that, though, she didn't make another appearance for a long time. A better-rehearsed Con-

stance might have gone skipping about with the
village maidens to fill in the interval between her
songs, but she'd serve the cause better by lurking in
the wings and keeping out from underfoot. She was
supposed to pop out and hand Dr. Daly the teapot
later on, but she didn't have to say anything, merely
drink her tea along with the rest and fall, like them,
into an enchanted sleep until it was time to wake
up and become unwillingly engaged to Cousin Frederick. That wouldn't occur until after the trio and
chorus at the opening of the second act.

Sarah wished she could have a session alone with
the book; it was hard to concentrate on her part while
she rouged cheeks and raised eyebrows. Jack Tippleton showed up at her table tonight, and allowed
her to convert him into a proper old country squire
without any protest. Sarah wondered if this was on
account of the tongue-lashing he'd got from Emma
at the dress rehearsal, or because Gillian Bruges
wasn't around to be impressed by his youthful vi-
rility or dismayed by the lack thereof. He'd given up
trying to impress Sarah Bittersohn, obviously.

Sarah couldn't have cared less one way or the
other. She had too many others lined up waiting for
her artistry. It occurred to her as she got toward the
end that Sebastian Frostedd wasn't among them.
Maybe he'd decided to do his own face tonight, now
that she'd set a pattern for him to go by; or maybe
he just thought he'd wait and avoid the crush. He
had lots of time, since he didn't appear until so late
in the first act.

She did think of sending one of Frederick's hired
guards to check on him, but then Ridpath Wale slid
into the chair beside her, so she asked him instead.
Ridpath only grunted, "In the men's room, most
likely," and demanded her full and undivided attention to his makeup, as well as a good deal of sym-
pathy for his heroism in going on with a damaged

ankle. He must not have noticed that he only limped when he'd made sure somebody was watching.

At last Sarah got everybody painted up who required painting and was free to mull things over while she put the finishing touches to her own cheeks and eyes. By the time Lady Sangazure sailed forth in her purple panoply, Sarah had both her face and her mind made up.

"Aunt Emma, I've been thinking. Once I've gone offstage, I'm not needed at all till after the intermission. Martha could manage that little business of handing Dr. Daly the teapot. That would give me a chance to dash back to the house and check on Gillian."

"Let me think." Emma hunted around on her bosom for the large gold watch that was one of Lady Sangazure's many accouterments and studied the time. "Yes, you could. You'd never be missed in the teapot scene, there's such a mob milling about then. You are supposed to be in the Marvelous Illusion number singing the soprano part with Aline, but that's a tricky one and you haven't had a chance to rehearse with the group, so perhaps it's as well you don't try. Besides, we all wind up shrieking at the tops of our lungs, and I don't suppose one shriek the fewer would matter. You'd have to be back here for your big number with Frederick at precisely nine thirty-five; but for heaven's sake don't cut it that fine or I'll have a heart attack and mess up the finale. Now if you forget your lines during the opening scene, just hurl yourself on Martha's shoulder and begin to cry. She'll clue you in. Ready? Places, everyone."

Chapter 18

The overture ended, the curtain parted. The bells
rang forth their clarion sound, and from the throats
of men and maids poured assorted sounds of rejoic-
ing. Sarah dithered in the wings. Martha squeezed
her hand. The male members of the chorus pro-
claimed for one last time that joy did definitely and
incontrovertibly abound, then made their exit. The
two Partletts entered, one downcast, the other per-
turbed, to show how wrong men can be about women.

Beginning in trochaic tetrameter and winding up
in iambic pentameter, Mrs. Partlett begged to know
the cause of her daughter's strange depression.
Constance delivered her agitated rebuttal, insisting
that all her blushings and palings, her long-drawn
sighs and tremblings of limb were nothing for a
mother to fuss about. Undeceived by this reply, as
what concerned parent would be, Mrs. Partlett motioned the girl choristers offstage and left Constance
free to make her plaint. She made it, all forty lines
of it, without a hitch.

From then on it was a piece of cake. Aunt Emma,
as a last-minute inspiration, had provided Sarah with
a beribboned basket, in the bottom of which lay a
well-marked script, and Emma's friend Millie, the
prompter, sat ready to hiss from the wings, but Sarah
needed none of their help. That was mostly because
she had hardly anything to say once Dr. Daly hove
into view bemoaning those long-gone, halcyon days

when love and he were well acquainted, little noting that he was still the object of a comely young woman's affections. Mrs. Partlett tried her hand at matchmaking, the effort came to nothing, Sarah fell sobbing on Martha's bosom and was led away to be comforted.

The applause from the audience was sweet, the hugs and hand-squeezings and slaps on the back from members of the cast back-stage were sweeter, but Sarah didn't pause to revel in their accolades. Dragging Frederick aside, she whispered, "Where's that policeman you hired?"

"Which one?"

"I'll take any one I can get. Quickly!"

"What's the matter?"

"I have to go check on Gillian, and I'm not going alone. And I have to be back here by half-past nine, so quit stalling and find me that policeman."

"I could—"

"You could not. You're on in about ten minutes. Frederick, move!"

Grumbling something about Cousin Mabel, Frederick moved. He was back in a moment, towing a man who'd been trying unconvincingly to look like a stagehand.

"Officer Murgatroyd," Frederick barked. "Take him, he's yours."

"Thanks," said Sarah. "Come along, please, Officer."

Officer Murgatroyd took a look at Sarah in her polka dots and curls—she'd have no time to change, of course, though she had remembered to park her basket backstage—and willingly followed her out to her car.

"I suppose I should have told Sergeant Formsby I was leaving the hall," he remarked as they got started, "only he told me not to bother him for anything short of murder."

"Yes, well, I hope it won't come to that," Sarah told him. "In fact, it may not come to anything at all. It's just that there's been another spot of bother."

She described the current bother, and he nodded. "I see what you mean. Too bad you had to leave the injured person by herself."

"I know, but there was nothing else we could do at the time. Miss Bruges refused to be taken to the hospital, her injuries looked to be ugly but superficial, and she wasn't in a bad state of nerves, at least not by the time we left. In fact, she seemed to be taking the incident more or less in stride," Sarah added rather caustically.

"It takes them that way sometimes. It's the shock. They get sort of I-don't-care, then they fall apart later. The victim's probably chewing her fingernails off up to the elbows by now, wondering if those two guys are on their way back to finish her off."

"I'm not sure but what she may have cause to wonder," said Sarah. "That's why I've been thinking we may be wiser not to drive straight up to the house. I don't want to turn this into a melodrama, but I'd as soon leave the car somewhere out of sight and slip into the house quietly."

"But if she's alone and okay, won't she get scared if we go sneaking in on her?"

"If she is, the chances are she's asleep and we can just sneak out again without her even knowing we were there. My aunt gave her something for her headache. Why don't we just drive by the house and take a peek in? I can pull up behind the neighbor's hedge."

"Can't do any harm." Officer Murgatroyd peeked, and not in vain.

"Say, is that your aunt's van in the driveway?"

"My aunt doesn't have a van. I think we're in business."

Sarah stashed her car, first dousing the lights,

then led Officer Murgatroyd at a quick scurry through the hedge and around behind the carriage house to the side door. The special door key she carried would deactivate the burglar alarm.

Warning each other not to make a sound, they went in. Luckily, Constance's costume called for soft, heelless slippers. Officer Murgatroyd solved the dilemma of Mrs. Kelling's polished floors by taking off his sturdy bluchers and carrying them in the hand that wasn't resting on the butt of his gun.

Sarah wasted no time checking the drawing-room sofa. She knew by now where Gillian would be. Beckoning the policeman into the breakfast room, she inched open the door that connected it to the big dining room. Through the crack they could spy somebody short and thin, in blue denim pants and jacket, examining one of Emma Kelling's silver epergnes with what looked like professional interest.

"Put that down." The voice was Gillian's, and she didn't sound a bit frightened. "And for Christ's sake, wipe off your fingerprints. Haven't you any brains at all? You're not lifting so much as a tooth-pick. We're not leaving one single sign that anybody's been here but me. When that bunch get back, they're going to find me on that couch just where they left me, nursing my goddamn eye. Did you have to slug me so hard, Lev?"

"You said we couldn't get away with any faking because the old dame knows too much about makeup."

That was the voice of a different male, and Sarah recognized it. The kind taxi driver who'd picked up Gillian after her mauling from the alleged car thieves and brought her safe to haven was back. "Besides," he went on, "I've been wanting to hang one on you for quite a while."

"Thanks, lover. I'll do the same for you one of these

days." Gillian sounded more sincere than usual, Sarah thought. "Come on, let's move it."

"What's the big rush?" That was the skinny one, nasal and whiney. "You told us the whole goddamn neighborhood's down at that show you were supposed to be in."

"What if they find they can't do it without me? I want that painting out of here pronto. Go ahead. One of you at each end."

Now all Sarah could see of Gillian and her crew was one pair of dirty bare feet. The man had been wearing heavy boots or running shoes with distinctive treads in the soles, she deduced, which Gillian had made him take off before he came in. There'd be no tracks in the carpets, no noticeable fingerprints, nothing to be missed because Ernestina was supposed to be already gone from the house. There'd be no locks forced, no burglar alarm sounded downtown because Gillian had been inside to shut it off and let in her henchmen without fuss or bother. She'd let them out again, turn the burglar alarm back on, and go back to being the stricken innocent. One had to give her credit for a well-planned operation.

"How the Christ did you get this goddamn billboard under here all by yourself?" the taxi man was grunting.

"That's my business," Gillian told him sweetly. "Just take it easy on that stretcher. One scratch and you're dead. We've got maybe a couple of million riding on this deal, remember."

"Says you. Where's it supposed to be coming from?"

"I have my connections."

"Who, for instance?"

"Think I'm fool enough to tell you? Look, you made out all right on that last job, didn't you? I don't remember hearing any complaints when you collected twenty thousand apiece for a couple of hours' work, and never a sniff from the cops, either. Isn't that one hell of a lot better than hustling Cadillacs out of parking garages?"

Sarah didn't wait to hear what the man had to say. She touched Murgatroyd's arm, motioned for him to stay put, and mouthed that she was going to telephone for reinforcements. He nodded, and she left.

Up in Aunt Emma's boudoir, with its heavy carpet and tight-fitting door, those downstairs couldn't possibly hear her using the phone. Nevertheless, Sarah kept her voice down as she described a robbery in progress at Mrs. Beddoes Kelling's house, and gave the officer at the desk the number and description of a van that was parked at the top of the drive.

"Officer Murgatroyd has them under surveillance right now. I should say your best plan would be to come along quietly and bottle up the driveway so the van can't get out. I don't believe they're armed, unless they have weapons in the van. They think they have the neighborhood all to themselves, you see. But for goodness' sake, if you do have to shoot, aim for the tires instead of the gas tank. What they're stealing is a very large painting worth a great deal of money. And please hurry!"

"We're on our way."

"Good. I'll go down and let Officer Murgatroyd know."

It was as well she went. Gillian's men already had Ernestina out from under the table and were wrapping her in two of the large, padded mats movers use. They must have brought the mats with them. A thoroughly professional operation.

Sarah could see both men's faces now. The taxi driver was easy to recognize. The smaller, thinner man had an oddly shaped head that was narrower from side to side than from front to back, and a nose like a knife blade. She'd know him again.

So would Officer Murgatroyd. He was being patient, like a good cop, his notebook out and his pencil busy scribbling notes of what they were doing and saying. He wouldn't try to arrest them alone, not now that he knew help was on the way. He'd let them take the painting from the house, making sure a robbery had been well and duly committed, leaving no legal loophole for them to escape through. The police of Pleasuance must have had lots of experience with clever criminal lawyers.

Now they were passing strong cords around the mats and tying them. Gillian was testing the knots, leaving nothing to chance.

"Okay, they'll hold. You know exactly what you're to do. No speeding, no funny stuff, no stopping except for traffic lights. Just get out on the pike and keep going till you reach the exit I've marked on the map, then stay to the right. It's a low wooden building with a big sign out front that says 'Fried Clams,' and a little one stuck on underneath that says 'Closed for the Season.' Watch your odometer; it's exactly two miles from the exit, on the right. Drive around to the back. There'll be no lights showing, but somebody will be expecting you. Here's the fake bill of sale. You're all set for gas and oil? You've checked the tires?"

"Yes, mother dear," said the taxi driver.

"No guns in the van, in case you get stopped and searched for any reason?"

The thin fellow snorted. "What kind of jerks do you take us for? We've got brains enough not to set ourselves up for a murder rap. Unlike some people we know."

"You keep your mouth shut." There was something in Gillian's voice that made Sarah and Officer Murgatroyd exchange startled glances. "I do nothing that's not an essential part of the operation."

"The hell you don't. You didn't say anything about wasting that old geezer when you roped us in to ferry the painting."

"Roped you in? That's a hot one. You've been pestering me for months to—look, we haven't got time for this. Just get out of here."

They didn't go.

"Okay," Gillian admitted. "Daventer wasn't part of the plan because I didn't know he was in it, for God's sake. He'd got laid up with gout or some damned thing before I managed to wangle my way into the cast. He'd never been to a rehearsal till Wednesday night. So all of a sudden here he is, reminding me we'd met in Newport at that house party where poor dear Mrs. Poofenwidget had her Rembrandt etchings stolen. So the same night poor dear Mrs. Kelling's going to lose her Romney, and where does that put me?"

"Couldn't you have waited till the next night and set somebody up, just in case?" asked the taxi man.

"No, I couldn't. It was then or never. Just like it's tonight or never for you guys to get this damned thing out of here. Will you quit stalling and go?"

"I want to hear more about Daventer," said the thin one. "What makes you think she'd have told him? I thought you had it all figured out she wasn't going to say anything to anybody, between your fake ransom notes and her not wanting bad publicity for the show."

"She'd have told him. He was her boyfriend. Anyway, it went off like a breeze. He cracked his skull on the bathtub, taking a leak in the night. Happens all the time. They cremated him this morning, for God's sake, and Mrs. Kelling's having some kind of memorial thing tomorrow. None of that would be happening if anybody suspected there was anything phony about his death, would it?"

"You ought to know." He really was a mean little devil, Sarah decided. "You've been lucky before, haven't you, Gillie?"

"I'll be lucky again if you don't get off my back, Sid. Go on, get moving."

"Right," said the taxi driver. "Come on, Sid, pick up the other end. So long, Gill. Get a good rest and don't worry about a thing. See you in New York."

He'd be seeing her again sooner than that, Sarah thought. She waited till Gillian had let the two men out the front door, gone back to the drawing room, and resumed her pose as resident invalid. Then she showed Officer Murgatroyd to a new post of surveillance from the library, left him to stand guard, and scooted through the hedge to her car. They must be almost to the intermission by now. She hadn't much time.

Still she didn't start her car. She'd better wait till the van got off. They might panic and try something foolish if they heard another motor turning over in a place they were supposed to have all to themselves. She didn't want to do anything that would jeopardize the police trap. On the other hand, she couldn't sit around here while Aunt Emma had that fit. Where were the police cars? She strained her eyes through the dark—not so very dark, since Pleasaunce was generous with its streetlights—but couldn't see them. She could hear the van starting, moving down Emma's drive, pausing at the bottom, turning—and driving away. The police weren't there.

Chapter 19

If Sarah had stopped to think, she might not have done what she did. But there wasn't time to think. She was due on stage in seventeen minutes, and Ernestina was on the way to New York. She gunned her engine and went after the van full tilt.

She wasn't fool enough to try ramming the other vehicle, her idea was to force it off the road. But how did one manage that? She tried blinking her lights and pulling up alongside. They thought, of course, she merely wanted to pass. And what was there to stop her? The road was deserted except for themselves; everybody else in Pleasaunce must in fact be at the show. Including those miserable policemen who ought to be here doing this instead of her.

She simply wasn't getting her point across. She stayed with them, edging closer. The taxi man, who was driving, turned for an instant to stare at her. She honked and edged closer. He slowed down for a second, then speeded up. She stayed with him, neck and neck.

This could get dangerous. She must do something, now, before they got going too fast. Deliberately, wondering, "My God, what's Max going to say?" she pulled half a length ahead and angled sharply to cut him off.

There was an open lawn, or what looked like one, beside them. Thinking, no doubt, to swerve around and get in front of this maniac, the taxi man took the van up over the sidewalk, ripping the side of Sarah's car with his bumper as he passed.

Little did he know Emma Kelling's neighbor was a bird-lover, and that the field had been let go entirely to those multiflora roses that provide such wonderful food and cover for wild creatures, and such tenacious vines and thorns to trap the unwary. The van stalled. The men jumped out, got snared by the roses, and were hopping around saying horrible things when the police cars at last arrived.

Sarah paused only long enough to shout, "They're unarmed and I'm late," then stamped on the gas pedal. Her car couldn't be too badly damaged, it was able to break every speed record the town fathers of Pleasaunce had ever hatched. She made it backstage just as the villagers were waking up. Aunt Emma was beside herself.

"Sarah! I was wondering if I'd have to fall in love with Frederick myself. Whatever kept you?"

"Gillian was—restless. I had to wait till things quieted down."

"What a bore that girl turned out to be. Of all times to throw an attack of the vapors. Was she all right when you left?"

"In excellent spirits and resting comfortably. Everything's under control now." It had better be. "Frederick and I go on right after the country dance, right?"

"Right. Here, let me straighten out your curls. You're all skewgee. Now, don't worry about a thing, Sarah. Just keep calm and collected. You do know your lines?"

"I don't have any spoken ones, do I? Only the song about the plain old man. And for the ensemble, I keep singing those bits and pieces about how my poor heart is blighted."

"Yes, yes, that's right. Now, be sure you sing loud and clear. It's still your number, don't forget. You mustn't allow the others to drown you out. And don't forget to be crying as you go on. Where on earth did Frederick get to?"

"I'm right behind you, Emma," said the plain old man. "Stop dithering, for God's sake. Everything's going like clockwork. Isn't it, Sarah?"

"Absolutely," Sarah answered loud and clear. "Not a fly left in the ointment. How does it feel to be engaged, after dodging women all these years?"

Rather to her surprise, Frederick grinned like a catfish. "Not bad. Got your tonsils greased for the main event?"

"I'm as ready as I'll ever be."

"No you're not. One of your cheeks is pinker than the other. You'd better give yourself a new paint job."

Sarah ran back to the makeup table and made some fast repairs. The act reminded her of the car. She hadn't even had time to assess the damage, and she shuddered to think what it might be. After having ached for Max all week, it was strange to find herself hoping he'd stay away long enough for her to get to the body shop.

Not that he wouldn't have done the same as she under similar circumstances, but he'd probably have managed to be more adroit about it.

"I do confess an anxious care my troubled spirit vexes." She'd be singing that soon, and meaning every word of it. Damn Gillian Bruges, or whatever her real name might turn out to be. Why couldn't she have been a nice young woman who liked to sing minor roles with amateur operetta companies, instead of a professional crook who preferred to steal their paintings? Well, on with the show. Sarah gave her apron a final twitch, took a dainty handkerchief from its pocket—trust Aunt Emma to think of everything—and prepared to enter sobbing.

Chapter 20

Sarah and Frederick got through their number with a creditable degree of panache, all things considered. They received their due meed of applause, but this was Emma Kelling's night, no doubt about that.

Lady Sangazure couldn't do anything wrong. When her voice at last broke down irrevocably, it happened during the number where her potion-induced adoration is spurned by the conscience-stricken Sorcerer and was admired by the audience as a magnificent piece of acting. When she finally gave her hand to Sir Marmaduke, she was applauded to the rafters. By the time she rode her high-wheeled bicycle onstage for her final curtain call, there couldn't have been an unstrained vocal chord left in the house. This was no swan song. It was a paean of triumph or, in Cousin Frederick's more picturesque phraseology, the neigh of ultimate victory from a great old war horse.

The stagehands finally had to ring down the curtain while the audience was still on its feet shouting, because Emma literally had not the strength to go out there again. She was collapsed into a chair backstage, swamped by a crush of Kellings and others who'd begun swarming to kiss her cheeks and wring her hands and tell her over and over again how totally, absolutely, devastatingly marvelous she'd been. Cousin Mabel had come prepared to air an alternate viewpoint but for once in her life couldn't get a word in edgewise.

In the midst of all the hoopla, a tall man with ruggedly handsome features, a wonderful head of dark, wavy hair, and a beautiful new necktie from Finland fought his way to the corner into which Sarah had been squashed by the mob.

"So," he growled into her false ringlets, "I let you out of my sight for a few days, and you run away to join the circus."

"Max!"

That was all Sarah got to say for quite a while. When she at last regained the free use of her lips, she had to ask about the Picasso, which was now in the complicated process of being repossessed by its rightful owner, about how he'd got here, which had been accomplished by bumming a ride with some cronies of Uncle Jem Kelling's, and about the state of his health, which he claimed to have been seriously impaired by being separated from the partner of his joys and sorrows.

"Oh," said Sarah. "Speaking of sorrows, I'm afraid I have another one for you. I banged up the car this evening."

"Were you hurt?" He anxiously began testing for damage, to Cousin Mabel's patent disapproval and Sarah's not very convincing protests of public embarrassment.

"Stop that, silly. I'm fine. It was just that they were getting away and I had to stop them somehow."

"They who?"

"The men in the van with Ernestina. I think we'd better get out of here."

"You and me both, *kätzele*."

They couldn't get near Emma, but they did manage to find Heatherstone and tell him they were going back to the house. Sarah collected her clothes but didn't bother to change. It would have been im-

possible anyway with all those people milling around.
Probably the whole cast would wind up wearing their
costumes home and there'd have to be a grand
roundup after the tumult and the shouting died. And
then perhaps they'd never be used again anyway, at
least not by the Pirates of Pleasaunce. No matter,
Emma had had her triumph. Sarah squeezed Max's
arm and they went out to see what was left of the
car.

It wasn't as bad as Sarah had feared, but it was
bad enough. There was a deep scratch running all
the way from the front righthand fender to the middle of the rear door. The front door would probably
have to be replaced entirely.

"But it still runs fine," Sarah insisted.

"That's nice," Max said somewhat grimly. "How
the hell did it happen?"

"I had to let him hit me. You see, I was trying to
run him off the road and he didn't seem to be getting
the point, so there wasn't much I could do but cut
right across in front of him. I tried to calculate the
angle so it wouldn't do too much damage, but it's not
easy in a situation like that."

"Jesus! You could have been killed."

"Oh no, I was quite sure I wouldn't get hurt. The
van was rather a flimsy-looking old thing, and we
weren't going fast. That was the point, you see, to
get him before he speeded up. And I knew they hadn't
any guns in the car, because Gillian asked them."

Max made some kind of noise. Sarah kept talking,
fast. "Anyway, I got them both, or at least the police
must have. Smack in the midst of Mr. Perkins's roses.
I couldn't wait to watch them getting untangled because I was due onstage in about five minutes by
then. Maybe we'd better just stop at the police station
and explain that I wasn't hit-and-running or anything."

"Maybe we'd better," Max managed to croak. "Want me to drive?"

"What's the matter? Don't you trust me?"

"Funny, aren't you? Dammit, Sarah, why didn't you call the police?"

"I'd called them, but they didn't show up in time. Somebody had to do something or we'd lose Ernestina. So I thought, what would Max do? and did it. So it's all your fault, actually."

"The hell it is. Who's Ernestina?"

"Aunt Emma's big Romney. You know, the one they have a faked copy of at Madam Wilkins's. You see, that's how I got to be Constance."

"Sarah, do me a favor?"

"I know, start at the beginning and go on to the end, then stop. Yes, darling. Here's how it happened."

She told him. She hadn't quite finished telling him when they got to the police station, but that was perhaps as well, since she had to begin all over again and tell her story to Chief Ruddigore, the officer on the desk, and anybody else who could spare the time to listen. Her audience was not large, much of the force was still down around the auditorium trying to straighten out the traffic, but she got rapt attention from all those present except the two surly young men in the lockup.

Ernestina was there, still wadded into her comforters and making the policemen terribly nervous. Strictly speaking, they ought to have kept her in protective custody until the trial that would surely be held. Because of her great value and fragility, though, they were going to send her home in the wagon when they went over to collect Gillian Bruges. Gillian was really Sergeant Formsby's collar, they explained, and the department liked to observe proper etiquette in such matters. Formsby would be along to collect his prisoner as soon as they could sort him out from the crowd leaving the show.

"There's no chance she'll get away, according to what you say, Mrs. Bittersohn?"

"None whatever, I'm quite sure. Her whole operation appears to be based on being Miss Innocence personified. In a way, I suppose it was a stroke of luck that you didn't get there in time to stop the van at the bottom of the drive. She might have heard the commotion and made a run for it."

"Nice of you to look at it that way, Mrs. Bittersohn. We meant to be there on time, though. What happened was, Officer Rupert in the lead cruiser got a bee under his glasses. It stung him on the right eyelid, causing him to lose temporary control of his vehicle and cream his left fender on the Beddoes A. Kelling Memorial Horse Trough, thus losing valuable minutes getting to the scene of the crime while he and his partner pried the fender off the wheel so they could back out."

"It's always the thing you least expect, isn't it?" Sarah answered. "I'd never have dreamed of a bee."

The chief said that was how it went, and complimented Sarah on her fast thinking and expert driving, though it was a darn shame about that nice car and he knew how Max must be feeling.

Max said bravely that cars could be fixed and he was just damned glad his wife didn't need to go in for repairs, too. Then Sarah said they'd better get back to the house before Aunt Emma walked into the library and found Officer Murgatroyd squinting through the door with his gun trained on Gillian Bruges, because Aunt Emma had already had enough excitement for one night; and they went.

It was as well they did. Dolph's Marmon was already parked in the drive, but no passengers were aboard. Sarah raised her eyebrows, gave Max a pleased nod, and rang the doorbell. Aunt Appie was the one who answered.

"Surprise! Didn't expect to find little old chickabiddy me playing doorman, did you? Max, how super-mellagorgeous to see you. I knew Mabel must have got her facts a wee bit twisted when she was telling me all those things about you and Sarah during the intermission. Mabel does have a hearing problem, you know, though she won't admit it."

"Hearing problem, hell!"

Dolph Kelling loomed behind, looking like the chairman of a society for the prevention of something or other, which in fact he might still have been, although his work with the Senior Citizens' Recycling Centers had given him a viable excuse to resign from most of his late Uncle Frederick's nuttier foundations.

"H'are you, Max. Good to see you back. Mabel hasn't got a hearing problem, what she's got is a listening problem. If it isn't something vicious, she just tunes it out. Where's Emma, Sarah?"

"Still receiving the plaudits of her multitudes when I left. She sent the Heatherstones on ahead, then?"

"Damned if I know. I haven't seen hide nor hair of 'em. We sneaked out during the curtain calls. Knew there'd be a mess in the parking lot once they all came charging out, and I'd never get the old Marmon through it. She doesn't take kindly to all that stopping and starting stuff. Beginning to feel her age, you know. Mary's been suggesting we might retire her to the Auto Museum and start thinking about a new car. One of those beach wagons or whatever they call 'em nowadays. We could haul stuff around, you know, take people for rides and all that. Damn good company, some of our workers."

"I'm sure they lead very interesting lives," said Appie. "One never knows what may turn up in a trash bin, does one?"

Sarah knew better than to answer that one. "Then who let you in when you got here?"

"Some young woman with a peach of a black eye," Dolph told her.

"You don't happen to know when Mrs. Heatherstone will be back, Sarah?" Aunt Appie broke in. "I thought of asking her for a piece of beefsteak to put on that poor girl's eye. It's the enzymes in the beef, you know. They draw out the swelling. Or is it the discoloration? Or both?"

"Or neither," Dolph snorted. "Old wives' tale."

"Well, dear, I'm an old wife, or was till poor darling Sam went to his well-earned reward."

"Reward? Huh, if he'd got what was—"

Sarah cut off the no doubt inflammatory remark Dolph was trying to make. "Never mind that now. I want to know what happened when Gillian opened the door."

"Gillian? Is that her name? How pretty. So old-world and quaint. Or should one say winsome?"

"Shut up, Appie," snarled Dolph. "What do you mean what happened, Sarah? She opened the door and we came in. What the hell was supposed to happen—beating of drums and fanfare of trumpets?"

"The burglar alarm didn't go off?"

"Of course it didn't go off. Why the hell should it?"

Because Gillian wasn't supposed to know how to shut it off in the first place, and must therefore have forgotten to reset it after she'd let the two men out with Ernestina, that was why. Sarah gave her cousin a pat on the shoulder.

"Thank you, Dolph. You've just struck yet another blow for the cause of justice and of right."

"Have I? Hot damn, I must go tell Mary."

"No, wait. We're going to hold a little ceremony as soon as Aunt Emma and a few more people get here. It will be formally announced then. Come on, Aunt Appie, let's go out to the kitchen and get things started for Mrs. Heatherstone. Dolph, you'd better come with us so you can tell us what we're doing wrong. Max will go and help Mary take care of Gillian. Max is awfully good at first aid, you know."

Max was also awfully good at handling an art thief who might by now have realized she'd made a serious blunder by opening that door.

Chapter 21

But Gillian was either unaware of her faux pas or didn't think anybody had caught it. Sarah, shepherding Dolph and Appie past the drawing-room door at quick march, heard Gillian acknowledging Mary's introduction of Max in a dying-away voice, apologizing for not being able to rise from the sofa and for being such a dreadful sight. She certainly must be by now. That was one part of the operation the taxi driver had carried through without a hitch, at any rate.

Appie in a kitchen was always a disaster. Sarah apologized mentally to Mrs. Heatherstone as she watched her aunt pulling the refrigerator apart in a luckily fruitless effort to find a piece of steak to put on that poor girl's eye.

Fortunately, Appie wasn't given much time to wreak her depredations. Emma breezed in triumphant, laden with bouquets that had been showered on her, followed by Mrs. Heatherstone, Frederick, the Tippletons again *en famille*, and Parker Pence, who appeared to have adopted a whither-thou-goest attitude toward Jenicot. Heatherstone was putting away the Buick and the Marmon, having naturally assumed Dolph and whomever he'd brought along with him would be staying the night even though the household had received no official notice to that effect. Mary hadn't called because she didn't think it was her place to, Appie hadn't because she'd started

202

to look for Emma's number and got sidetracked by finding some of her son Lionel's baby pictures, and Dolph hadn't because why the hell should he? Emma knew he wasn't going to punish either himself or the Marmon by driving all the way back tonight.

So the rooms were ready, the Heatherstones only too eager to take over their appointed duties, and Sarah free to herd Dolph and Appie back to the drawing room, just in time for the thrilling denouement. Chief Ruddigore, who'd once seen Emma in *The Pirates of Penzance* and knew what she would expect of him, led the procession. Next came Officer Ruthven, handcuffed to the taxi driver. Third came officer Roderick, handcuffed to the skinny fellow with the knife-like nose. Fourth and fifth respectively came officers Rupert and Richard, ever so carefully bearing a large, flattish object wrapped in heavy matting. Bringing up the rear in style came Sergeant Formsby in his best suit with a red carnation in his buttonhole, dangling an empty pair of handcuffs and looking remarkably pleased with himself, as well he might.

Gillian could hardly pretend to be other than shaken, nor did she try. She cringed, she sobbed, she tried fainting, but there was no way she could get out of admitting she'd shut off the burglar alarm she wasn't supposed to know how to work. Not with Adolphus Kelling declaiming that the damn thing hadn't emitted so much as a goddamn tinkle when she'd opened the door to him and his ladies, and Mary backing him up. Nobody, after taking one quick glance at Mary Smith Kelling, would ever dream of doubting her word about anything.

So Gillian did the next best thing, claiming she'd been coerced into it by her two assailants, exhibiting her battered countenance as *prima facie* evidence and citing horrendous threats of further maulings if she'd refused to cooperate.

At that, the skinny one with the nose made a statement. The only words in it deemed inoffensive enough to record were that Gillian was a liar. He was prepared to embellish this theme with an apparently inexhaustible string of expurgations, but the taxi driver contrived by a lot of yelling to make him shut up.

"The gist of the matter is," the taxi driver told Chief Ruddigore pleasantly, "my co-worker and I appear to have been made the victims of a plot. We'll be glad to make a full statement as soon as we've been allowed our constitutional right to confer with our attorney. Won't we, Sid?"

Sid growled something that might pass for an assent and fell silent, which was a good thing because Aunt Appie was already talking seriously of finding some soap to wash that boy's mouth out with.

"I don't believe you'll have to hold up the proceedings while you wait for their statement," Sarah told Chief Ruddigore. "Officer Murgatroyd has been taking notes for quite some time. Would you put on your shoes and come in, please, Officer Murgatroyd?"

Officer Murgatroyd already had his shoes on and his notebook well filled. He began reading, to as attentive an audience as Emma Kelling had ever assembled. When he got to the part about Charlie Daventer, Emma stopped him.

"That's enough. I can't stand to hear any more. Chief Ruddigore, get that woman out of my house this instant, and never let me set eyes on her again."

There were no more steams and vapors. Gillian Bruges caught the look in Emma Kelling's eye and decided she'd be safer in jail.

Sergeant Formsby made the formal arrest, as was his due, but gave Officer Murgatroyd the honor of escorting Miss Bruges out to the patrol wagon. He was followed by officers Ruthven and Roderick, still manacled to her confederates, and by officers Rupert and Richard, the former to unlock and relock the cage, the latter to do the driving. Formsby himself stayed behind for a few minutes with Chief Ruddigore to assist in the unwrapping of Ernestina and get Max to check her over and make sure she was in pristine condition before leaving her in the possession of her lawful owner.

"Put her down cellar or somewhere," Emma told Max and Dolph after the policemen had finally cleared out. "I'll never be able to look at her again without seeing Charlie Daventer's blood on her hands."

"Emma, that's hardly a sensible attitude to take," Jack Tippleton protested.

"Sensible? A fine one you are to talk about what's sensible. Bringing that creature into the cast, into my home—"

"Mrs. Kelling, he didn't," Jenicot protested. "Gillian just showed up with a letter of introduction from somebody or other."

"Which she probably wrote herself," Parker interjected.

"Anyway, Daddy only—"

"Proceeded to make a fool of himself after she got here," Jenicot's mother finished for her. "Emma, if you were planning to serve drinks, I believe I'd like a Manhattan."

"A Manhattan?" Tippleton stared at his wife in astonishment. "But, Martha, you never drink Manhattans."

"How would you know what I drink? You never stay home long enough to find out."

Emma Kelling was too experienced a hostess to let somebody else's family row develop in her drawing room. "I think Manhattans are a splendid idea. A toast to Broadway and the Pirates of Pleasaunce. We'll all have a Manhattan, Heatherstone, then people may have what they like, provided they fix it themselves."

She tossed aside the mohair throw Gillian Bruges had been using as a prop for her act, and eased herself down on the brocade cushions. "One feels as if this sofa ought to be exorcised or something before we use it again, but frankly, I'm too tired to bother. Come here, Max, and sit with me. It's good to have you back, but I must say I don't know what I'd have done without Sarah all to myself this past week. She and Frederick, of course; but then dear old Fred's everybody's prop and mainstay."

Dear old Fred was propping Martha Tippleton at the moment. She'd turned a cold shoulder to her husband's peacemaking attempt and settled herself beside Fred on a love seat facing Emma. Jenicot crouched on a hassock at her mother's feet, looking woebegone. Parker Pence hovered nearby like a lost sheep until Mary Kelling kindly took him in tow and steered him over to the generous spread Mrs. Heatherstone had got ready before she left for the show, knowing full well Mrs. Kelling wouldn't be coming back alone. Dolph joined them and began questioning Parker on his plans for the future. Jack Tippleton went to the bar and mixed himself another drink, not a Manhattan.

Sarah was snuggled at the other end of Emma's sofa, with Max's arm around her. Heatherstone fixed a plate of little sandwiches and brought them over to her.

"Here you are, Sarah. I noticed you didn't eat a bite before the show. You must be starved by now." He caught Max looking at him in some surprise and said rather stiffly, "We've known her since she was a baby, sir."

"And she's been lucky enough to know you," Max replied. "Thanks for looking after her. By the way,

Jem sends his best. I'm supposed to kiss Mrs. Heatherstone for him. Do I have your permission?"

"I'm sure she'll be pleased to get the message." Heatherstone and Max exchanged man-to-man grins, then Heatherstone went on passing sandwiches.

Emma Kelling was getting her poise back. "You know," she remarked after she'd finished the first half of her Manhattan, "what puzzles me most are all those silly notes that kept popping up. If she intended to steal Ernestina all the time, why did that horrid woman go through the mockery of pretending she wanted to extort money from me?"

"Stalling for time," Sarah answered with her mouth full. "She knew she wouldn't be able to get Ernestina out of the house until tonight, because this was the only time she could be sure the coast was clear. She reasoned that as long as you were expecting a ransom demand, you'd hang on to the hope of getting Ernestina back, and not call in the police."

"But there was a ransom demand, or sort of one," Frederick protested. "And what about that silly business of locking you in the potting shed? Most of it was kid stuff, so how does it tie in with what went on here tonight? I don't know what Max thinks of the way Gillian set this up, but it strikes me as a pretty damned slick operation."

"I couldn't agree with you more," said Max. "That woman's a pro, and so are the guys she worked with. Therefore we come to a certain conclusion, which I'm sure Lady Molly of the Yard has already drawn. Tell 'em, Sarah."

"Yes, dear. It seems to me the obvious explanation would be that two different sets of people were working on this affair. Gillian's team were professionals, as Max just said, but the others were the rankest of amateurs. I believe that while Gillian knew perfectly well what the others were up to, they hadn't a clue about her and her gang. Another interesting differ-

ence is that while Gillian wouldn't stop at anything—I'm sorry, Aunt Emma, but there it is—the
others were, on the whole, almost timid about what
they were doing."

"What do you mean, timid?" Parker Pence asked
her.

"Perhaps that's not quite the word," Sarah con-
ceded. "I'd have said courteous if they hadn't stuffed
me into that old burlap sack and locked me in the
potting shed. And even that didn't amount to a row
of pins because I was able to get right out again."

Sarah took another of the little sandwiches. "I'm
sure it was the other group who took Ernestina out
of her frame and hid her under the dining-room table. They did take good care of her, you know, in an
amateurish sort of way. They didn't risk taking her
out of the house. When I found her, she'd been carefully covered with newspapers. I suspect these had
come straight out of Aunt Emma's own wastebasket
because the amateurs hadn't thought to bring any
padding with them. The professionals did, as you
know. As for the notes, I think the amateurs got a
bit carried away with their own cleverness."

"What do you mean?" Mary Kelling asked.

"Well, the messages were pretty silly, to begin with.
They were lettered in a somewhat crude attempt at
calligraphy except for the first one. That was a newspaper clipping thumbtacked inside the frame from
which Ernestina had been taken. Only one of the lot
actually mentioned money, by the way, and the sum
demanded was so absurdly small in proportion to
Ernestina's value that it made no sense. Another
note came in a box of flowers. The one that was stolen
from me in the potting shed had been hooked to the
outside of the library screen with a couple of paper
clips."

"Paper clips?" exclaimed Jack Tippleton.

"Yes, it makes you think at once of Ridpath Wale,

doesn't it? He has sort of a thing about paper clips, I discovered, the way some people do about bits of string or elastic bands. I'm wondering now if that particular note hadn't been a subtle attempt to implicate Ridpath, of which the conspirators quickly thought better, and if the attack on me was made for the purpose of getting the false evidence away."

"Then I gather you've ruled out any possibility that it was in fact Ridpath," Jack persisted, "and that he'd left evidence against himself that had to be retrieved."

"Yes, I've ruled Ridpath out," Sarah assured him, "considering that Gillian tried to do him in by unscrewing one of the stair treads down from the trapdoor at the dress rehearsal. He was lucky to get away with a banged-up ankle."

"How dreadful," gasped Emma. "Why did she do that?"

"I don't know if it was just a piece of general nastiness to build up the extortion threat or if she had something personal against Ridpath."

"But she'd have wrecked the show and ruined her own plot to get the painting away. Where would I have found another Dr. Daly?"

"Bear in mind that whatever else Gillian may be, she's also a capable and experienced performer. I'm sure she must have sung with other Gilbert & Sullivan groups, and had some man all lined up who knew the part and could step in for Ridpath. If she'd found you a last-minute substitute, she'd have been your fair-haired girl for life, wouldn't she?"

"I suppose so," Emma admitted. "And after what she'd done to poor Charlie!"

"Were there any other notes, Sarah?" Mary Kelling asked quickly.

"Oh yes, they came thick and fast. One was inked on the tapes of Aunt Emma's bustle. Interestingly enough, Gillian also used the bustle as a post office, but hers was typed and skewered on with Uncle Bed's pet paper knife, which she'd pinched out of the library."

"Sarah claimed it said, 'Kick me.'" Emma remarked in a rather stiff tone.

"Well, the message was pretty nasty, and I wasn't about to go broadcasting it all over the theater. Sebastian Frostedd was standing right there, and at the time he was one of my prime suspects. I may say that our amateur kidnappers did a neat job of setting him up for having been the one to put the sleeping tablets, or whatever they were, in the Slepe-o-tite the night they stole Ernestina."

"They what?" cried Martha Tippleton.

"That was their neatest bit of work. They made sure Aunt Emma, the Heatherstones, and I all were slumbering peacefully while they were down here wrestling Ernestina out of her frame."

"That must have taken some doing," Max observed, glancing up at that immense rectangle of gilded gesso.

"I'm sure it did, but at least they weren't faced with the problem of getting her out of the house. I doubt that they'd ever have dreamed of doing such a thing. I'm not sure whether they thought it didn't actually count as stealing if they left her in the house, or whether they hid her under the table because it was such a perfect hiding place. In fact, I'm wondering if they decided to take Ernestina instead of the Renoir or something else that would have been easier to pinch just because she happened to be a perfect fit between the handles."

"What an interesting idea," Aunt Appie observed brightly. "It would never have occurred to me to take measurements."

"Yes, well, I doubt whether it would have occurred to Gillian Bruges, either. I suspect she may have had quite a different target in mind when she first wormed her way in here, but happened to hear our amateur masterminds planning their perfect crime and decided to turn it to her own advantage. Those men were asking her tonight how she managed to get Ernestina under the table. She just smirked and told them she had her methods. Obviously her method was simply to sit back and let the other team do it for her. Frederick and I proved to our own satisfaction this afternoon that two people could work the trick easily enough, once they got the knack. Especially if they were a couple of husky youngsters who played tennis a lot and had crawled under the dining-room table when they were kids, the way I used to do. What did you want the five thousand dollars for, Jenicot?"

Jenicot Tippleton was obviously not cut out for a life of crime. She'd begun to fall apart even before Sarah gave her the final nudge.

"It was for Mummy," she sobbed. "I wanted to buy her a f-facelift."

"A face-lift?" roared Frederick Kelling. "What the flaming blue blazes would a beautiful woman like Martha want with a face-lift?"

"To make her look y-younger. Daddy was being so s-silly, chasing after all those g-girls, I was hoping—"

"Oh, Jenny!" Martha Tippleton clearly didn't know whether to laugh or cry. "Emma, I'm sorry. She's too old to spank and apparently too young to think. Jenicot Tippleton, if you think for one second anything on the face of this green earth would keep your father from chasing after every new skirt that flutters by, then you may as well think again. You've caused a great deal of heartache and bother, and I insist you apologize to Mrs. Kelling this instant."

"Oh I do! I do!"

Jenicot literally flung herself at Emma Kelling's feet. "And please don't blame Parker. I b-bullied him into it. Besides, he'd do anything for Mummy. He's crazy about her. It j-just"—she had to stop and blow her nose on a cocktail napkin—"seemed like such a good idea at the time."

Emma Kelling's face remained stony. Sarah Bittersohn knew why.

"Aunt Emma, it's not fair to blame Jenicot and Parker for Charlie Daventer's death. Gillian Bruges is a ruthless, vicious, scheming woman who deliberately wormed her way into the show for the express purpose of committing a robbery in this house. What they did with Ernestina gave her a ready-made plot, but if that hadn't been the case, she'd have gone after something else. She murdered Charlie Daventer simply and solely because as soon as he laid eyes on her, he recognized her as having been at that place in Newport when the Rembrandts were stolen, and reminded her of that fact. Gillian knew that if she went ahead with her plan, Charlie would put two and two together, and she'd be caught. And she wasn't about to give up a fortune for an old man with the gout."

"Yes, I see."

Emma Kelling reached out and stroked Jenicot's bright hair. "It's all right, Jenny. Everybody makes the stupid mistake of trying to arrange somebody else's life at one time or another. It can't be done and shouldn't be tried. It took me a long time to find that out. You and Parker have been fortunate enough to learn your lesson early. I hope you'll remember."

"How could we forget?" Jenicot blew her nose again. "I feel like such a fool."

"Me, too," Parker mumbled. "If there's anything in the world we can do to make up—"

"There is." Emma Kelling was riding high again. "You may as well know I've made up my mind to retire from the Pirates of Pleasaunce. I'm too old to sing, soon I shall be too old to direct. As of now, I'm taking you two on as my apprentices. I intend to teach you everything I know, and I expect the pair of you to carry on in my place when I'm gone."

"To you from failing hand she throws the torch," Dolph amplified. "Be yours to hold it high."

"You tell 'em, dear," said Mary like a loyal wife.

Parker and Jenicot looked alarmed and said they'd try. Frederick said they'd damned well better. Jack Tippleton, who'd been sulking in the background, continued to sulk.

Max, who hated to leave any loose ends dangling, asked his wife, "How did the knockout drops get into the Slepe-o-tite?"

"I expect Bonnie and Clyde here can answer that better than I."

"It wasn't knockout drops," Jenicot protested. "It was just four of Mummy's sleeping pills, two for each jug because you're not supposed to take more than two at a time and we didn't want to poison anybody. We knew about the Slepe-o-tite because Parker and I have been coming here ever since we can remember, like Sarah, and we always liked to hang out with Mrs. Heatherstone in the kitchen. She's nice."

"And my grandmother had given us this box of liqueur cherries to bring to Mrs. Heatherstone," Parker added, "and we figured they'd eat them that night and they'd take away the flavor of the sleeping pills, so we held on to them till that day. And then we happened to run into Sebastian Frostedd and asked him to deliver the chocolates. We thought it would look less suspicious if they didn't come straight from us."

"Don't you mean because you knew perfectly well he'd pass them off as a present from himself?" Sarah asked him.

Parker gave her a nervous grin. "Well, there was that possibility. So anyway, how we worked it was, Jenny gave me the pills and I brought them to the rehearsal in my pocket. They were gelatin capsules, actually. I took them apart and had the powder in a little envelope. Gillian had stuck me for a lift, but I pretended to remember at the last minute that I didn't have my car and dumped her on Sebastian. Actually I'd let Guy Mannering drive it away. He and a friend of his had this live raccoon in a carrier they were going to let loose. I'd better not say where. So I watched my chance and sneaked into the cellarway. I knew I could keep an eye on the kitchen from there. The door's got a peephole in it I guess maybe Mrs. Heatherstone doesn't know about."

"Good heavens," said Emma, "I do. I'd totally forgotten. Young Bed did that with an ice pick when he was nine years old, playing I Spy with Walter. I was none too pleased when I found out, but their father thought it was funny, so we never plugged it up. I'm surprised you never discovered it, Sarah."

"I never liked that cellar much," Sarah admitted. "Walter used to tease me with horror stories about the man-eating water bugs that lived down there."

"What rogues those boys were," said Emma fondly. "Go on, Parker, what did you do with the sleeping powder?"

"Waited till Mrs. Heatherstone put the milk on to heat and went into the butler's pantry with the dessert, then ran in and dumped it into the pan. I stirred it around so nobody would get more than a fair share. We were as careful as we could be, honestly. Then I ran back down cellar and waited for Jenny."

"Who was hiding somewhere out in the back yard by the time I got back from visiting Cousin Frederick, I'll bet," said Sarah. "I had a feeling somebody was watching me."

"I was behind the coach house," Jenicot admitted, "and I'll bet I was a lot more scared than you were. Parker let me in as soon as you got inside, before you could set the alarm, then we had to wait around till we were sure you'd had time to feel the potion's power. We watched through the peephole when you were getting the cups and the jug so we knew you'd drunk it. Then we got Ernestina out and hid her."

"That must have been quite a job," said Max. "How did you manage?"

"Well, you see, we knew it wasn't going to be so hard as you might think," Parker admitted. "Once when Mrs. Kelling was babysitting me, I watched the man cleaning Ernestina, and found out she was only held in with a few screws. I noticed he had both long ones and short ones in his box, so when he went off to have a cup of tea with Mrs. Heatherstone, I took out the long ones and put in short ones. I thought it would be fun to see Ernestina come popping out when they went to hang her back up on the wall, but she didn't. So I knew the screws were still too short and all we had to do was lift her away from the wall without unhooking the chains, and poke the stretcher loose from the frame."

"But we were very careful," Jenicot insisted. "We didn't hurt her a bit. We'd meant to put a clean sheet over her but I forgot to bring one and we didn't think it would be right to pinch one out of your linen closet, so we used newspapers."

"And then we had to go back and hide in the cellar for the rest of the night, till Mrs. Heatherstone unhooked the burglar alarms to let in Guy for the scenery," Parker went on. "We were going to say we were out jogging if anybody saw us, but nobody did, so we got home okay."

"Sarah," said Max, "if any of our neighbors ever ask you to baby-sit their kids, for God's sake tell them no. All right, now that we've settled that little question, how did the Bruges woman manage to get into Daventer's place that night? Did she swipe his keys?"

"No, Charlie's keys were all present and accounted

for," Frederick told him. "However, he had given out keys to several of his friends. I imagine Gillian contrived one way or another to get hold of one of those."

Frederick didn't say whose. He didn't have to. Martha turned her head and gave Jack Tippleton a look of utmost contempt. Then she stood up.

"Thank you, Emma, for a quite remarkably interesting evening. Kiss me good night, Jenny."

"But I'll see you back at the house."

"Not at that house, you won't. Not tonight or any other night."

Jack Tippleton goggled. "Martha, what are you talking about?"

"I'm all through talking, Jack. I'm acting. If you want a divorce, I shall see to it that you have ample cause. However, it doesn't seem to matter much these days one way or the other. Ready, Fred?"

"Been ready these past forty years. You can forget about the face-lift, Jenny. I like her the way she is."

"You're leaving me for Fred Kelling?" Jack couldn't seem to grasp that it was actually happening. "But he's—" He was what? Elderly, yes, but so was Jack. Rich, respected, and certainly a damn sight more faithful than her husband had ever been. "But he's ugly!" Jack blurted.

"Is he?" said Martha. "I hadn't noticed. Good night, everyone."

It was a superb exit line, but of course the actual departure got messed up with a lot of hugging and kissing and assurances from Frederick to Jenicot that she'd be welcome as the flowers in May at their house as soon as he and Martha got rid of the present tenants and fixed the place up a little. Only Jack Tippleton got left out of the celebration.

Being Jack, he had to get the limelight back somehow. He did it by swiping the Sorcerer's own last, best line: